MOUNTAIN BIKE MANIA

The #1
Sports Series
for Kids

MOUNTAIN BIKE
MANIA

LITTLE, BROWN AND COMPANY

New York ⌇ An AOL Time Warner Company

To John and Ann

First Paperback Edition

The characters and events portrayed in this book are fictitious. Any similarity to real persons, living or dead, is coincidental and not intended by the author.

Library of Congress Cataloging-in-Publication Data

Mantell, Paul.
    Mountain bike mania /Paul Mantell. — 1st ed.
        p.   cm.
    Summary: Sixth-grader Will is looking for an after-school activity, but when he joins the mountain biking club, his old friendships and values are challenged.
    ISBN 0-316-14355-3 (hc) — ISBN 0-316-14292-1 (pb.)
    [1. All terrrain cycling — Fiction.   2. Schools — Fiction.
3. Friendship — Fiction.]   I. Title
PZ7.C458Mo   1998
[Fic]— dc21   98-24050

10 9 8 7 6

COM-MO

Printed in the United States of America

MOUNTAIN BIKE MANIA

Will Matthews stared at the television screen and stuffed another handful of candy-coated popcorn into his mouth. On the screen, a girl and a guy in exercise outfits were leading an aerobics class. Everyone looked in perfect condition, even the students.

Will glanced down at his own stomach. Not me, he thought. I must have gained at least ten pounds since school started!

This business of coming home after school to an empty house was not turning out so great. Ever since his mom had landed her new "high-powered" job at the software company, Will's life had gone totally downhill. With his dad already working long days at the law firm, it meant that from two-thirty, when he got home from school, till five-thirty or six, when his mother got home, nobody was around. His

1

dad usually didn't walk in the door till six-thirty or seven.

Will was an only child, but until now, he hadn't minded. In fact, he had always felt kind of superior to all his friends when they complained about their brothers and sisters. But now he was jealous of them. It would be cool to have somebody around to argue with in the afternoon. Anybody!

Will grabbed the remote and started channel surfing. He couldn't stand looking at those perfect people for one more second. But, as always seemed to happen in mid-afternoon on the weekdays, there was nothing good on any channel.

Will flicked off the set and got up. He stretched, then went upstairs to his room. The empty popcorn bag stayed on the couch.

Upstairs, he pulled the chair out from his desk. His computer was already on. He'd played *Crash Coogan* for an hour before turning on the TV. The computer's clock read 4:30 P.M. He'd wasted two hours but still had another hour or so to go!

Will thought about tackling his homework, but he had a free period tomorrow morning. He could do it then. Since his mom wasn't around to prod him, he didn't force himself to work.

Glancing around the room, his gaze fell on the telephone. Maybe he'd call Danny Silver. Danny had been his best friend ever since first grade. Pulling the phone toward him, Will punched in Danny's number, only to get a busy signal. After a minute or two, he pushed the redial button. Still busy.

He's probably on the Internet, Will said to himself. Sitting down at the computer, he logged on to see if his hunch was correct.

While he waited for the connection to be made, Will checked himself out in the full-length mirror on the back of the door. Twelve years old. Not bad looking, if you didn't count the wire-rim glasses and the extra ten pounds. Lucky thing he didn't have to wear braces. No zits . . . so far. Short dark hair, blue eyes, nice face, like his mom's, dark eyebrows like his dad's. He was okay, he guessed.

Will wasn't all that popular at school, though. He was shy and didn't make friends easily. He and his family had moved here to Montwood seven years ago, and he'd more or less stuck with the same few friends the whole time. That was fine in elementary school, but now he was in sixth grade.

Middle school was different. Most of the kids at Hopgood Middle were from other neighborhoods, and he didn't know them even to say hi to. As for his old friends, they were all too busy to get together during the week. Too much work, too many clubs, teams, and lessons, blah, blah, blah.

Will would watch the other kids get picked up after school every day by their parents. Then he would ride the ten blocks home by himself, pedaling his rusty old three-speed bike. It was the only exercise he ever got anymore. Will wasn't much for sports, and he wasn't about to start working out with those perfect people on the TV show.

He sat back down and clicked his way around the Internet. Danny wasn't logged on, and neither were any of Will's regular chat room buddies.

Will felt like screaming. There was nothing to do!

Being a "latchkey" child was the pits! Oh, it hadn't been so bad during the summer, when there were plenty of kids around the neighborhood. Now they were all too busy, and he was alone.

Heaving a deep, heavy sigh, Will put the computer screen to sleep, then went downstairs to get his book bag. How much lower can you go? he thought, trudging sadly down the stairs. When homework is the most entertaining thing to do, your life is truly pathetic!

Will's mother came home and found him staring vacantly at the Home Shopping Network, his schoolbooks scattered on the floor around him.

"Will!" she gasped, grabbing the remote and shutting off the TV. "Is this how you've spent the entire afternoon?"

"I finished my homework!" he protested, snapping out of his trance. "Most of it, anyway."

"Well, that's good," his mother said, softening a little. She took off her coat and hung it up, then held up a shopping bag. "I brought home dinner!" she said brightly. "Chinese food."

Will groaned. He had once liked Chinese food, back in the old days, when they didn't eat it for dinner three times a week. Now he was about sick of it. "Thanks, but I'm not hungry," he said.

"That's because you've been gorging on junk

food!" she retorted, grabbing the empty popcorn bag. "Did your father buy you this stuff?"

"He bought it for himself," Will corrected her. "I just got to it first."

"Well, that's not acceptable, young man," she said sharply, heading off into the kitchen. "We're going to have a talk about it over dinner!"

Uh-oh. The dreaded "talk over dinner." This is not looking good, Will thought miserably.

And he was right, too. When his dad got home, they all sat down at the table together. Will kept quiet, hoping his mom would forget to bring up the subject. But no sooner had his parents exchanged the news of their jobs with each other than his mother started in: "I'm concerned about Will, Bob. He's got nothing to do after school, and he's just staring at the television for hours and hours and eating all the junk food you bring home."

"I only ate the caramel popcorn!" Will protested.

"Hey, I bought that for myself!" his dad said, instantly annoyed.

"I was hungry!" Will explained defensively. "There was nothing good in the refrigerator because you never go shopping anymore. And what was I supposed to do, wait for you two to get home? I would have starved to death!"

His parents exchanged a funny look — half guilty, half furious. "Look, son," his father said. "I know it's been hard on you, with both of us working full-time. But you're old enough now to find a way to entertain yourself away from the TV. . . ."

His father's voice petered out as Will started drumming on the side of his plate with his fork. "Okay, what is it that's eating you?" his dad asked.

"I just don't understand why Mom has to work all day, every single day. It leaves me stuck in the house!"

"That's the way my job is structured, honey," his mom said apologetically. "Look, Will, we knew there would be a difficult period of adjustment for you."

"We just didn't know how difficult or how long it would be," his father finished.

"Would it help if we hired a baby-sitter — I mean, a child-care worker — to be here with you?" his mom asked.

Will rolled his eyes and bit down on his tongue. He didn't want to say anything he'd regret, but they'd talked this all out before. A baby-sitter? He was twelve years old, for Pete's sake! What were they going to do, pay some fourteen-year-old to be his friend?

"What about after-school activities?" his father suggested. "Some sports team or other. You look like you could use a little exercise, after eating all *my* caramel popcorn."

That forced Will to crack a smile, and the momentary spell of anger was broken. "I hate sports, and you know it," he said to his dad. "I'm just no good at them."

"Oh, come on, now," his dad challenged him. "How can you say that? You've never even tried out for a team. Maybe you're better than you think you are!"

"Yeah, right," Will snorted.

"Just give it a try — that's all I ask," his dad said. "If you don't make it, we'll figure out something else."

Will just sighed. There was no use appealing to his mom. She'd just agree with his dad — especially since Will didn't have any better ideas.

"Okay," he mumbled. He carried his plate to the sink, rinsed it, and put it in the dishwasher. Then he went straight up to his room, flopped down on the bed, and thought about tomorrow. He dreaded trying out for a sports team. He wasn't a good athlete, didn't like competition, and was not exactly thrilled about the possibility of humiliating himself and maybe even getting hurt!

No, tomorrow was not going to be pretty.

"You okay, kid?"

Will was on his knees, not sure if he was going to hurl or not. "I think so," he breathed, his stomach still turning.

"Guess you didn't pace yourself well enough," the coach said, chuckling and patting Will ever so lightly on the back. "That half-mile run will take it out of you if you aren't careful."

"Did I make the team?" Will asked, not even looking up.

"Um, er, I . . . well, let me put it this way. You need to work up your strength and endurance. Then you can start working on your speed. Why don't you come back next year at this time and we'll see how far you've come?"

"Sure," Will said, staggering to his feet and trudging off. "Thanks anyway."

9

It was his third tryout of the week. On Tuesday he'd been flattened by a football that hit him right between the eyes. "Gotta get those hands up and catch that thing!" the coach had advised.

Then on Wednesday, he'd totally humiliated himself on the soccer field when he'd tripped over his own feet and accidentally knocked the ball into his own goal. "Take a break, there, kid," the coach had said. "Are you sure you've played soccer before?"

Now he'd been defeated on the track, where he'd been trying to keep up with a bunch of long-distance runners. Will forced himself to his feet and shuffled over to the bike rack. He retrieved his beat-up old three-speed and started pedaling home. By the time he got there, his stomach had more or less stopped heaving, and his ears weren't popping anymore.

He guessed he'd live. But he wasn't going to go through another day like this one. He'd tried out for three teams, and already he was the laughingstock of the whole sixth-grade locker room.

Will walked up the driveway and entered the house through the garage. It was almost five o'clock.

Tonight at dinner, he was going to lay it all out for his parents. He'd tried out for three teams; that was enough. Three strikes, and he was out. Now they had to let him play couch potato. That was all there was to it.

"Look, maybe those just weren't your sports," his dad offered lamely at dinner when Will had finished telling his sad, painful story. "You still need some kind of physical activity. Don't they have a lacrosse team or a golf squad? Maybe tennis . . ."

"Bob," his mom said in a tight voice, "I think Will's been through enough."

Go, Mom! Will thought, breathing a sigh of relief. "Thanks," he said gratefully.

His mom nodded. "I think you've had enough of trying to succeed at sports. But there are *other* things in the world, you know. . . ."

Uh-oh, Will thought. Here it comes.

"There are clubs and other after-school activities. Right, Will?"

"I guess so," Will said glumly, wishing it weren't true.

"How about the debating team or the chess team?" his dad suggested, brightening at the thought.

"There must be some noncompetitive clubs, too," his mother added, giving his dad a sharp look. "What about arts and crafts?"

"Mom!" Will moaned. "I stink at art!"

"Now, now," his mother said. "What about that nice vase you made for Grandma that time?"

"I was seven years old," Will reminded her. "And it was supposed to be a dish."

"Well, it was a very nice dish," she insisted. "An interesting shade of greenish brown, I remember."

"Yeah, 'cause I messed up the glaze," he said. "Mom, do I have to?"

"You have to do something," his dad said, striking the table with his hand. "If you'd rather go out for something else —"

"No, that's okay," Will interrupted him before he suggested anything worse. "Arts and crafts will be fine."

"There, it's settled," his mom said, with a pleased-looking smile. She kissed him on the head as she got up, then made for the kitchen. "You'll see, honey —

12

you'll get into it after a while. Just give it a chance." The door swung shut behind her.

"At least I don't have to *try out* for arts and crafts," Will said to his dad. "I still haven't got my appetite back from this afternoon."

"I'm sorry, son," his dad said softly, looking down at his own plate. "I'm sorry about all of this. But you can see how important this new job is to your mother. It means so much to her. She loves being your mother and spending time with you, you know that. But just like you'd go crazy if she was all you had in life, she'd go crazy if she didn't have something besides you. Understand?" Will nodded. "Try to make the best of it in arts and crafts, okay? At least until you find something you really like."

"Okay, Dad," Will said. He meant it, too. He really did want his mom to be happy.

But he wanted to be happy, too. And he was pretty sure that going to arts and crafts classes after school wasn't going to do the trick.

2

Will sat on his stool in Arts and Crafts Workshop, staring at the object he had made. Around him, the other students, some adults, some kids, were equally absorbed in their work. It was a good thing, too, Will thought. It kept them from noticing the monstrosity he had created.

He'd already forgotten what he'd originally intended it to be. Right now it was best described as a brownish gray blob, vaguely in the shape of a bowl, made of clay but with bits of colored glass and beads sticking out of it. He decided that since it was totally useless, it was not a craft piece but a work of art. He wondered if anyone would ever pay to see it. Maybe if he made it even uglier, until it was really spectacular. . . .

14

On the other hand, no. Arts and crafts was not for him — he'd known that right from the start. He glanced up at the clock on the wall. Still ten minutes to go before class let out and his mother came to pick him up on her way home from work. Here at the art school, they still had clocks on the wall. At his regular school, they'd wised up a long time ago and gotten rid of the clocks, so students wouldn't stare at them instead of paying attention in class.

Maybe if I put it on a base, it will look like a vase, he thought. He kneaded a small amount of clay into a pedestal and gingerly mounted his work of art on it. A moment later, it toppled to one side and hit the concrete floor with a loud, embarrassing splat. His creation now looked like a multicolored pizza. He shook his head sadly.

At dinner, his masterpiece sat dead center on the dining room table, for everyone to admire. Neither his mom or dad said anything beyond "Oh, wow!" and "Interesting . . ." Will dug into his chow mein and tried to think how he could get out of arts and crafts and back in front of his TV and computer.

"Will," his mother said as she poured him some more milk, "maybe arts and crafts wasn't such a good idea. It's not that I don't like your . . . your work . . . but maybe your father and I have been on the wrong track here."

"Huh?" Will looked up and paid attention. This sounded promising. "What?"

"Obviously," his dad said, "it's not working for us to force the issue. I think we have to lie back a little and wait for a solution to present itself."

"Are you saying I can stay home and watch TV?" Will asked, not quite believing it — and not sure he even liked that idea anymore.

"Let's not get back into bad habits," his mother said. "Will, let's explore some other ideas. For instance, how about we make a list of things you like to do."

"Okay," said Will, relieved at least to be out of arts and crafts.

"What activities do you like best?" his dad asked.

"Not sports," Will was quick to say. He thought for a moment. "I guess . . . well, Danny went hiking at camp last summer, and he said it was pretty cool."

"Good!" his dad said, smacking the table the way

he always did when he was excited. "Hiking — what about it, honey?"

"Well, there are lots of trails in the hills outside of town," his mom said. "But how's he going to get there after school?"

"Well, maybe the school has a hiking club or something," his dad suggested.

But Will shook his head. "Danny asked about one when school started. They had one last year, but the guy who organized it graduated to high school. And no one seems to have wanted to form it this year." He didn't add that Danny was too shy to try to do that himself. His parents, who knew Danny well, didn't ask, anyway.

"Why don't you give Danny a call and see if he wants to go with you on Saturday?" his dad said. "I'll drop you off and pick you up, and you guys can go, just the two of you."

"Okay!" Will said, jumping up to get the phone. Finally they were getting somewhere!

Danny Silver picked up the phone himself. "Hello?" he said in his funny, nasal voice. Danny always sounded like he had a cold or something. It didn't bother Will — at least you knew it was Danny

17

when he picked up the phone. But a lot of kids made fun of him for it, and for the thick black glasses and weird clothes he wore.

Will often felt like giving Danny some fashion advice — not that he himself got into that stuff. But he knew Danny would take it the wrong way. Danny thought designer labels were stupid and a waste of money, and he didn't care whether the cool kids liked him. Not trying to fit in made him unpopular at school, but it was one of the things Will liked best about him.

"It's me," Will said, knowing that Danny would recognize his voice. "Wanna go hiking Saturday? My dad will drive us there and back."

"Sure!" Danny said eagerly. "I haven't been hiking since the summer. I'm getting really out of shape."

"Me, too," Will said. "That's kind of why I called."

"Huh?"

"Never mind. I'll tell you when I see you."

"Man, I hope the weather stays good," Danny said. "Listen, I've got some astronaut food I can bring, and stuff like that. If you have binoculars, bring them along, okay? In case we see any deer or bears or birds or stuff like that. Oh, and you'll need your backpack, because I always bring a lot of water, 'cause you never know, and it's heavy and I'll collapse if I have to carry it all myself."

Finally Danny ran out of breath and came up for air. He always did that when he got excited about something. It never failed to make Will laugh.

"Relax, we'll figure it all out before we go," Will said. "We'll pick you up about nine, okay?"

"I'll be ready!" Danny said, and hung up.

"Okay, we're on!" Will told his dad as he came back into the dining room. "Now, what about after school? If I get some exercise on Saturdays, can I veg on the weekdays?"

"We'll see," said his dad, scowling. "We'll see."

That meant no, as Will well knew.

"Don't worry, Will," his mom assured him. "You'll find something you like. I'm sure of it."

Will sighed. He wished he was as sure as she was.

"Hey, where's that astronaut food? I feel like I've lost ten pounds already!" Will plopped down on the grass at the side of the trail. Exhausted, he threw off his backpack, fished a bottle of water out of it, and took a long drink. Danny sat down beside him.

"Drink a lot of water — that's the secret," Danny advised. "You can get really wasted otherwise."

"Too late." Will wiped the sweat out of his eyes and looked around. It was a hot, sunny day, and the hills around Montwood were green and beautiful. The air smelled like pine needles, and birds were calling to one another across the treetops. Way up above, a big bird — a hawk or buzzard — glided along on the warm air currents, looking for a meal.

They were sitting at the junction of two trails. Their trail sliced across the hillside and was fairly level. The up-slope side was lined with low growing brush. The other trail, a narrow, rutted track, zigzagged down the hill, flattening out only here in the clearing. The second trail met the first near some brush.

Will was just wondering what had made the ruts in the second trail, when Danny interrupted his train of thought.

"This was a great idea of yours, going hiking up here," Danny said.

"Well, to tell you the truth, it wasn't exactly my idea. My parents —"

"Say no more," Danny interrupted with a wave of his hand. "It really bites, being a latchkey kid."

Will nodded. He knew that Danny was speaking from the heart. His dad had died when he was only five — before Will had even known him — and his mom had to work two jobs. Danny was alone a lot of the time. Will had always felt sorry for him, but now he was glad to have a friend who could really understand what he was up against.

"How can you stand it?" Will wanted to know. "I mean, you must watch more TV than anybody!"

"Nah," Danny said, tossing a pebble at a nearby stream. "Most days I just read. You know, at the library."

"Yeah, that's right. I forgot." Will frowned.

That was one big difference between Danny and him. Danny was a real brain. He would have gotten all A's without even trying, but he always read up on all his subjects to learn more. It was like he wanted to know everything there was to know about everything.

Will wished he felt that way, but the truth was, reading made his brains start to bubble after about half an hour. And the thought of going to the library made him break out in hives.

"My mom and dad are never going to lay off me until I find some activity to do after school," Will said, tearing open a pack of freeze-dried astronaut ice cream. "Want some?"

Danny took a piece, and they lay there on their backs in the grass by the side of the trail, under the shade of a big pine tree that swayed in the breeze. "What time is your dad picking us up again?" Danny asked.

"Three," Will said. "But it's only one-thirty. We can rest for a few minutes before we head back. Man, my whole body hurts." He chuckled. "My dad would say, 'It's good pain!'"

"There is no good pain," Danny said. "Unless it isn't yours." And they both laughed.

Just then, there was a loud cracking noise as the underbrush near the junction of the two trails parted. Suddenly three people on mountain bikes came barreling through and landed on the steep, rutted trail. Their faces had wide grins plastered on them. One of them was yelling, "Ya-hoooo!" at the top of his lungs.

"Look out!" Will yelled. He and Danny rolled and dove to get out of their way. The cyclists never even slowed down, though one gave a little wave to the boys, laughing loudly. In seconds, the bike riders were out of sight, and the clearing was silent again.

"What jerks!" Danny muttered. "I can't believe it! They almost killed us!"

Will's heart was racing, and he, too, had been scared. But there was another feeling rushing through him, mingling with the fear.

Exhilaration. Those cyclists were as free as could be!

Will saw them again in his mind's eye, speeding down the mountain trail on a bicycle with the wind in their faces, smiling, laughing, shouting — and he could see himself with them.

Will stared at the trail where the bikes had disappeared, and the thought hit him: That's it — that's what I want to do! I want to mountain bike!

It had to be the coolest thing to do on the face of the entire planet!

3

Can you believe those idiots?!" Danny said, incensed, as he picked himself up and dusted himself off. "Look at all this mud they got on me!"

"Chill, Danny," Will told him. "We're okay, that's what counts. I'm sure they just didn't see us in time. We were lying down in the high grass, after all."

"What were they doing off the trail, anyway?" Danny continued. "They're supposed to go single file and watch out for hikers and horses. But none of them do. They're nuts, I'm telling you. Mountain biking is strictly for jerks."

Mountain biking. Will had heard of it, lots of times. But he'd never actually seen mountain bikers in action, rocketing down a trail at top speed. Again, he pictured himself doing it. Awesome!

"I don't know, Dan," he said. "I think you're just mad, that's all. You'll get over it."

"*This* time," Danny grumbled, hoisting his backpack onto his shoulders. "Come on, we've got to get back. Your dad will be waiting."

They walked down the trail in silence, each thinking his own thoughts. Will's were all about the brand-new mountain bike he'd soon be riding — that is, if he could talk his parents into it.

"I figured out what I want to do after school," Will told his mom and dad that night at dinner. Tonight it was home cooking, for a change. His dad had put together a big salad, and his mom had made lasagna.

"Oh, yeah? What's that?" his dad asked, looking curious and hopeful.

"I want to mountain bike!" Will said.

"Mountain bike?" his mother repeated. "On a mountain?"

"Mom," Will said, rolling his eyes at her ignorance. "Mountain biking means you bike down all kinds of trails, not just on mountains."

"Is it safe?" she wondered aloud. "I don't want you getting into anything dangerous."

"I think it's a great idea!" his dad said enthusiastically. "And don't worry, Maggie. Millions of people are taking up mountain biking. According to everything I've heard, it's safe so long as it's done properly."

"Well, I'd want to know lots more about it first," she said cautiously. "Can't you just bicycle around town, Will?"

"Mom, it's not the same thing," Will protested.

"Well, who would you be biking with?" his mother wondered. "I don't want you going by yourself. Does Danny go mountain biking?"

"Not a chance," Will replied, shaking his head. "It's not his thing. But I'll bet there are kids in school who do. Maybe there's even a club or something."

"Why don't you check and report back to us," his dad suggested. "Mountain biking sounds like a fine idea — lots of exercise and being outdoors — but you get all the particulars first, and let us know, okay?"

"Okay!" Will said excitedly. He could see himself

now, sailing down the mountain trail on his hot new bike!

That Monday at lunchtime, Will went into the school's main office and approached Ms. Henshaw's desk. Ms. Henshaw was the school secretary. She knew everything about everything that was going on at the school — or at least how to find out.

"Ms. Henshaw," he began, "I'd like to —"

"Will Matthews, right?" she asked, smiling at him through her granny glasses. "Ms. Milligan's class?"

"That's right," he acknowledged. "I'd like to find out whether there's a mountain biking club after school."

"Mountain biking?" she repeated, thinking for a moment. "Yes. They meet outside the gym entrance after school on Mondays, Wednesdays, and Fridays."

"Do you know who's in it?" he asked her.

"I couldn't tell you that offhand, but the president is Gail Chen. Do you know her?"

"Eighth grader?" he asked, picturing a tall girl with almond eyes and black hair in a ponytail.

"That's her," Ms. Henshaw said. "She's senior class treasurer as well, and head of the yearbook committee. I don't know how she gets it all done."

"Do you know where I could find her?" he asked. But just then, the bell rang for fifth period, and Ms. Henshaw got up.

"Sorry, Will, but I've got to take care of some things for the principal. Why don't you just show up at the gym entrance after school? That's where the club meets." And she was gone, before he could say okay.

At the end of the day, Will rushed to the gym and through the doors to the outside, only to find that it was pouring rain. He waited around for a while, but nobody showed up. Everyone was just running outside to get picked up by their parents.

"Dang!" Will said after a few minutes, realizing that nobody was going to show up. He went back through the hallways to the front door, then made a mad dash for his old bike. He was soaked through before he even got to it, and by the time he made it home, he was a wet rag. A disappointed wet rag.

He'd have to find Gail Chen tomorrow, one way or another.

In the meantime, he knew enough to approach his parents for their agreement.

"The club meets three times a week after school," he told his mom and dad over supper — pizza this time. Even his dad had decided enough Chinese food was enough. "Every Monday, Wednesday, and Friday."

"Sounds great!" his dad said. "Three times a week? You'll be back in shape in no time!" Then his face grew concerned. "I guess you'll be needing a new bike, eh? It's gonna cost a bundle, I'll bet."

"Not so fast, Bob," his mom interrupted. "Do you know anything about the kids in the club, Will?"

"Well, I didn't exactly get to meet them," he admitted. "It was pouring, so nobody came to the meeting. But the president is this eighth-grade girl who's the class treasurer and writes for the yearbook and stuff."

"Well, that says something!" his mother said, sounding impressed and a bit surprised. "I'm glad to hear that there are some older kids involved. Good students, too, it sounds like."

"So can I join?" Will asked, pressing his case.

"What about Tuesdays and Thursdays?" his mother wanted to know. "If you're going to be out biking three times a week, I want to make sure you get some work done, and some reading, on the other two days."

"Okay, okay," Will agreed with a sigh. "I'll come home and do my work, I promise."

"Oh, no," she said. "If you're here, you'll be sitting in front of some screen with a bag of junk food in your hand. I want you to stay at the town library and wait for me to pick you up."

"Mom!" Will moaned in complaint. "Three hours in the library? I'll —"

"Never mind," she said, cutting him off. "If you finish your homework, you can read a book or use their computers. Besides, Danny's always there, isn't he?"

That's true, Will thought with relief. And the library computers did have one or two games, as he recalled. "Okay. It's a deal," he said, offering his hand for her to shake. "Two days a week at the library, three days a week on my new bike!"

"New bike? Now, Will, is that really necessary?" his mother asked. "What's wrong with your old one?"

"Dad!" Will said, enlisting his father's help.

"It is a little old and beat up, Maggie," his dad put in. "And after all, we are bringing in more income these days. I think we ought to encourage this new interest of Will's."

"Oh, I guess you're right," she said, smiling. "As long as you get a lot of use out of it."

"Believe me, Mom," Will told her. "I definitely will."

"All right, then. It's settled," she said.

Will smiled as she gave him her hand to shake. A deal was a deal. There was no way they were getting out of it now! And how bad could two afternoons a week at the library be, anyhow?

Hey — maybe he'd even read a book!

It was during lunch on Tuesday that Will found Gail Chen. She was in the back of the auditorium, meeting with her yearbook committee. Will had seen a notice about the meeting on the bulletin board. And he had snuck out of the cafeteria without a pass, because he figured that no aide or teacher would give him one without ten minutes of explanation.

Gail was leading the meeting, it seemed. At least she was doing most of the talking. She had a big smile and braces, and seemed really likable. Just watching her made Will smile, she was so animated and energetic.

He waited impatiently for the meeting to break up. When it finally did, he went up to her and said hello.

"My name's Will Matthews," he said. "I'm interested in the mountain biking club."

"You're kidding!" she said, widening her eyes.

"Uh, no, I'm not," he said, confused. "Why?"

"No, I mean, that's great! That's fantastic! We need some new blood."

"Blood?"

She tsked and rolled her eyes, then giggled. "You know, like, new people? Like you! Are you in sixth grade?"

"Uh-huh. Is that okay?"

"Sure! Fantastic. Gotta break 'em in young."

"Um, how many people do you have?"

"Only six," Gail said. "It's sad. Last year we had eleven, and it was great, but four kids graduated and one moved away. But if you join, that'll make seven! So, like, you have to join."

"I do," he said, smiling. "Who are the other kids in the club?"

"Well, there's Candy and Mitch McGeachie. They're twins — you might know them. They're sixth graders. And Steven Barrad, he's in seventh. Then there's Juliette Travis, who's in my year, and me. Oh, and Ace." She made a face. "How could I forget him?"

"Ace?"

"Ace Diamond. His dad owns the cycle shop downtown."

"Wow. What's he like?"

"You don't know him?" Gail shrugged. "Oh, well. He's different. You've gotta take the good with the bad, I guess."

"Huh?"

"Some people think he's the greatest thing since

33

sliced bread. Me? Well . . ." Gail glanced at her watch. "Listen, we've only got, like, thirty seconds, but . . . do you have a bike?"

"A mountain bike? No. Just an old three-speed."

"Forget it. You need a new bike, like, now."

"Now?"

"By like, tomorrow. We meet after school by the gym door and go out for a ride. Can you have a new bike by then?"

"Maybe," Will said uncertainly. He sure hoped he could. "What kind do you think I should buy?"

Just then, the bell rang. "I'm going to 309. You?" she asked.

"I'm in 111. I'll walk you to the stairs."

"Okay." She picked up her book bag, and they walked up the aisle to the swinging doors at the back of the auditorium.

"First of all, go to Diamond Cycle," she said. "There's a guy who works there in the evenings. Julian's his name. He's about nineteen, and he knows, like, everything there is to know about bikes. He'll tell you what you need to get."

The noise in the hall was deafening as five hundred students talked at once. Will yelled to make himself heard. "Julian at Diamond Cycle?"

"That's it. See you tomorrow!" Gail yelled back, and climbed the stairs with a wave.

Well, thought Will, continuing on down the hall. It looked like he was in the mountain biking club. And he didn't have to try out, either. Best of all, tonight he was going to get his parents to take him to Diamond Cycle and buy him a brand-new, first-class mountain bike!

4

Diamond Cycle was not a huge store. But there were bikes hanging everywhere: from the walls and ceilings, from pipes and wires. The place had the feel of a jungle full of bicycle trees, ripe with tire fruit. Will had to wade his way down the aisle, brushing the swinging tires out of his path.

At the end of the path stood a big wooden counter. Behind the counter stood a college-age guy with a dark brown ponytail. His grease-stained bowling shirt had the name Julian stitched on the pocket.

"Hi," Will said, coming up to Julian with his parents right behind him. "I'm Will Matthews, and this is my mom and dad. Um, Gail Chen sent me to you. She said you'd help me pick out a bike and stuff."

Julian grinned and nodded. He had a huge gap

between his two front teeth, but his smile was so infectious that it made Will and his parents smile, too. "Excellent," he said. "You came to the right place. Mr. and Mrs. Matthews, nice to meet you, too. You tell me what your budget limit is, and I'll get you the right bike."

"Well," Will's dad said, looking down uncomfortably. "I'll tell you, I couldn't help notice the prices of some of the bikes as we came in . . ."

"Tell you what," Julian said. "Let me show you the pre-owned bikes first. Most stores don't have them, but you can save a lot that way. More bike for the money, you know?"

"Aren't the new ones better?" Will asked, dismayed.

"Not necessarily," Julian said with a shrug. "Sometimes you can pay the same amount for a better quality used bike as you would for a lower-end new bike. And remember, you'll still need some other stuff to go with it. Luckily you don't need a new bike to get the most out of mountain biking."

Will looked up at him, surprised. "You don't?"

"Nah, it's not about how cool the equipment is," Julian said. "Some people get into that, but it's not like you have to. Mountain biking's da bomb diggity. It's about going out with a gang of your friends, riding around whatever trails you can find, getting dirty, and having a blast."

He took them in back, where there was another, smaller showroom, this one for used, or "pre-owned," bikes.

"We refit and refinish all these before we sell them," Julian said. "So it's just like getting a new bike, for about two-thirds the money. And we're the only store that sells pre-owned bikes. Most places don't bother, so you'd have to find one at a garage sale or through the want ads."

"Whoa, look at this one!" Will said, gravitating to an all-chrome bike with metallic red trim and decals that rested on its kickstand by the far wall.

"See?" Julian said, grinning again. "Who says you have to spend more money to have more fun? Yeah, I fixed this one up last week. Pretty good paint job, if I say so myself. New brakes and cables, new wheels."

"How much is it?" Will's dad asked.

Will held his breath when Julian quoted the price.

Only when he saw his father nod his head and smile did he let it out.

Julian wheeled the bike away from the wall and put the kickstand up. "But before we sign on the dotted line, let's see if it fits. No sense buying a bike that's too big for you. In fact, it's dangerous. You can lose contact with the ground, and that would not be good. You need to be able to put a foot down to steady yourself. There, get up on that seat, Will."

"It fits fine," Will said, ready to grab his bike and go. He loved it already. It was perfect. He could see himself on it, flying down the mountain trails at top speed, the sunlight glinting off the chrome. . . .

"Mmmm, you're right," Julian said. "Okay. You guys want to buy it?"

Will looked hopefully up at his parents.

"Son," his dad said, with a big smile, "ride it safely."

"It's yours, honey," his mom agreed.

"Yes!" Will cried triumphantly. "All right! I can't believe it!" He could hardly wait to get his new — er, pre-owned — bike home. He was going to ride it to school first thing in the morning, and by afternoon, he'd be off on the trail!

"Yo, Julian! You sold my bike!" The voice came from the doorway. They all turned to see a boy who must have been fourteen but looked seventeen. He wore a black leather jacket, torn jeans, and black army boots. He had two earrings in one of his ears and long black hair brushed back and slicked down. "You said you were gonna fix it up for me!"

"Ace!" Julian said, stiffening. "Hey, man, I did fix it up for you. Now you don't have to pay your father back for the damage you did when you took it without his permission."

"I just borrowed it!" Ace corrected him. "I was trying it out to see if it ran right."

"Yeah, right," Julian said, rolling his eyes. "Be glad I saved your bacon this time, and don't do it again."

Ace looked away and blinked, as though he was just noticing that there were other people in the room. "Hey, don't you go to Hopgood Middle?" he asked Will.

Will nodded. "Sixth grade. I'm Will Matthews. These are my parents."

"Hi," Ace mumbled, then turned back to Will.

40

"Nice to meet you. Enjoy the bike." He gave Will a nod, shot Julian an angry look, and walked back out of the room.

"Whoa," Will breathed. "Now I see what Gail meant about him."

"He's some piece of work, all right," Julian said. "Tell you the truth, I don't think his dad wants him riding the new bikes. Ace rides them kind of hard. Don't get me wrong — he's a great biker. He does stuff on a bike nobody else around here can do."

"Not even you?" Will asked.

"Me? Nah, I'm not that good. I'm more into fixing them up, you know? Getting them in perfect running condition." Julian wiped his hands with a greasy rag, then motioned for them all to gather around him.

"Okay, now I'm going to give you your first lesson in mountain bikery. This" — he pointed solemnly at the bike — "is a mountain bike. It's different from a regular bike because it goes anywhere. Look at these big, fat tires. Good traction, good padding, takes a pounding. Look at this frame. Strong but lightweight, for when you need to carry it. Shock absorbers to keep you from feeling the pain.

41

"These are the derailleurs. They help shift the gears. The idea of shifting is so you can keep a steady pace. That way you don't tire out. So you want to find the most comfortable gear for flat riding and then adjust from there."

He went on to show Will and his parents how to shift gears with his thumbs as he rode. Then he taught them how to brake. Twenty minutes had gone by when Mr. Diamond came in, scowling.

"Julian," he said. "There are four customers out there waiting for help. I don't mean to rush you, but . . ." He gestured frantically, gave Will and his parents a little smile, and ducked back out.

"I'd better wrap this up," Julian said, not seeming too worried or the least bit hurried.

"If you need to help someone else, go ahead," Will's mom offered.

"Yes, you've been more than kind to take so much time with Will — and with us. I feel like I got an education!"

"Me, too," Will's mom agreed.

Julian grinned. "Well, Gail sent him. So I had to treat him right." He gave Will fist fives and ruffled his hair. "Look, man, you already wear glasses, and

42

that's actually an advantage here, since you won't need goggles."

"Cool!" Will said, smiling. "I'm not used to thinking of them as a plus."

"Yeah, and I assume you've already got a helmet, yes?"

"Yes," Will said.

"Good."

"What about biking clothes?" Will asked.

"Will, we're already spending enough for today," his father counseled.

"But I'm gonna look like a dork on this great new bike with my regular clothes!"

"You're wrong about that one," Julian said, shaking his head. "Mountain biking's not about what you wear. It's about how you ride. Don't worry, not all the kids in the club at Hopgood wear cycling gear."

"They don't?" Will didn't quite believe this. Anytime he'd watched bikers on TV, they'd been wearing skintight, shiny outfits, and so had the bikers who'd nearly run him and Danny down.

"Nope. Gail doesn't, for one, and she's the club president. Look, forget about it for now. Trust me. On the other hand, you are gonna want knee and elbow pads, and good gloves, too. Trust me on this one, folks. He needs protective gloves."

"We'll pick them out while you ring us up," Will's dad said as they went back into the main showroom. "And thanks again, Julian. You've been great."

"Yes, indeed," Will's mom agreed.

"Thanks, Julian," Will said.

"Hey, come on in anytime for some free pointers," Julian said. "Don't worry — Mr. Diamond won't fire me for being slow. He knows I'm good at what I do."

He gave Will a wink and a big, gap-toothed grin.

The hours flew by until two-thirty the following afternoon. Will went and got his bike from the rack by the school athletic field. It was easy to spot — the shiniest, coolest-looking one, as far as he was concerned.

He walked it over to the gym doors, and there was Gail Chen, waiting with two other girls for the rest of the club to show up.

"Hi!" She waved, motioning him to hurry over. "This is Will, everybody. He's our newest member. Will, this is Juliette Travis, and this is Candy McGeachie."

"Hi," Juliette said, nodding to Will. She was already sitting on her bike, her blond hair tied back, and her helmet tilted back on her head, unfastened for now. Neither she nor Gail were wearing biking outfits, just jeans tied up at the ankles and old sneakers.

"Hiya, Will," Candy said with a wave and a grin. "We know each other from French class," she explained to Gail and Juliette. "Isn't Mrs. Dumont fun?"

Will was a little surprised at her friendliness. Candy and her twin brother Mitch were really popular kids. Everyone always wanted to sit with them at lunch. Come to think of it, Juliette was head cheerleader, and her boyfriend was the quarterback of the school's football team. This was much more of an "in-crowd" than Will was used to hanging out with. When Will had heard they were in the bike club, he wasn't sure what to expect. But Candy was making him feel like one of them already, and he relaxed.

"I like when Mrs. Dumont goes like this." He pursed his lips, like he was a fish, the way Mrs. Dumont did when she was teaching them how to pronounce certain French words. Candy giggled, and Gail and Juliette joined her.

"Where's Mitch?" Will asked Candy.

"Mitch? He's probably hanging out with Ace, as usual," Juliette said.

"Mitch, like, worships Ace," Gail said with a sigh.

"So does Candy," Juliette added.

"I do not!" Candy said, blushing and giving Juliette an elbow. But Will could see from the way they all giggled that it must be true.

Just then, Mitch and Ace, along with another boy, came down the path, walking their bikes. Ace was wearing dark blue and silver biking gear from head to toe. His leather jacket was slung over both shoulders. He looked totally cool, and confidence oozed from his every pore.

The other two boys' outfits didn't suit them quite so well, but they still strutted as if they were on top of the world. One was a very tall boy with a buzz cut, and the other, with blond hair down to his shoulders, was Candy's twin brother Mitch.

"It's the three stooges," Juliette quipped, her eyes twinkling. "About time, you guys."

"Hey, we had to get changed, right?" Ace said.

46

"Right," the tall boy agreed. "Gotta look good out there. All new outfits for the new season."

"Steve Barrad, this is Will Matthews," Gail introduced them. "And Ace Diamond. Mitch you already know. Will's the newest member of our club, everyone, so help him get used to everything, okay?"

"Sure thing," Steve said, giving Will a nod and a smile.

"Hey!" Ace said, suddenly recognizing Will. "You're the kid who bought my bike!"

"Well, technically, it wasn't exactly *your* bike. . . ." Will fumbled, suddenly feeling a little panicky.

"Ha, ha! Hey, just kidding," Ace said, grinning and throwing an arm around Will's shoulder. "No hard feelings. I'll get over it. In fact, check out the replacement!" He showed off his new bike — a gleaming green "Mean Machine," as the decal read. It was a hot bike, all right. "Right off my dad's rack. I'm testing this baby out for him. Oh, yeah — and welcome to the club, Will." He showed Will a complicated handshake. "That's how we do it, okay?"

"Sure," Will said, happy Ace wasn't still sore about the bike.

"And if you need any help on the trail, I'm there — anytime, all the time."

"Thanks, Ace."

"Okay," Gail said. "Now that everyone's here and acquainted, let me go over our schedule for the week. Today we're going out to Shepard Lake Trail —"

"Aw, come on," Ace interrupted her. "Forget that — it's too easy. Flat as a pancake. Why can't we do some hills?"

Gail shot him a look. "We have a beginner with us today," she said pointedly. "So I thought we'd start him off easy, till he's used to his new bike and understands how we do things."

Ace clicked his tongue and shook his head, but he didn't argue any further.

Gail ignored him and continued. "Then on Friday, we'll do the ski trails on Slide Mountain."

"Yeah, that's more like it!" Ace commented, satisfied.

Will could barely contain his excitement. He was glad they were starting slow. But a large part of him, like Ace, couldn't wait to barrel down a steep slope with the wind in his face and his bike in full flight.

"Well, let's get going," Ace said. "I can at least get some speed practice."

"You'd better not," Gail warned him. "You know Shepard Lake Trail is full of hikers and horses." Ace didn't reply, so she turned to the rest of the club. "Okay, bike check," Gail said, and they all dismounted to begin looking over their bikes.

"This is a routine we do every time before we go out," Gail explained to Will. "We have a safety checklist: skewers must be tight, quick release levers pointed to the rear, so they don't snag on anything. Tires pumped up, brakes working properly. Helmets fitted snugly. Kit on board . . . who's going to carry the kit today?" she asked, hoisting a small day pack.

"What's in the kit?" Will asked.

"First aid," Gail told him. "Along with tools, spare inner tubes in case one of us gets a flat, loose change in case we need to make an emergency phone call. Stuff like that."

"I didn't know you had to be that prepared," Will said.

"Well, not so much for today," she explained. "But when we go farther from town, like to Slide

Mountain or the reservation, it could be crucial." She gave the kit to Mitch, who had raised his hand, volunteering to carry it. Then she looked up at the sky. "Last minute check of the weather . . . looks good . . . and we're ready to go!"

She threw a leg over the bike and hauled off across the athletic field, heading for the road that led to Shepard Lake. Ace turned his bike around to follow her. "I don't know why she always has to lead," he grumbled. "It's like having a scoutmaster watching over you."

"Yeah," Mitch said, nodding. And Steve seemed to agree as well, although he didn't say anything. They all took off, one after the other, following Gail. Juliette and Candy came after, and Will brought up the rear.

"Don't worry," Juliette called out to Will over her shoulder. "If you fall too far behind, we'll stop until you catch up!"

Will waved to signal that he'd heard. Soon, he fell into a comfortable rhythm behind the other bikers. As they rode, through the heart of town and out into the hills, he began getting used to his new bike. Remembering Julian's advice, he practiced shifting gears and braking.

Soon they came to the dirt road that wound around the lake. The road snaked in and out, following the curves of the land. The leaves were falling all around them as they rode. The sun, low in the sky, glinted through the trees at them. Will squinted into the brightness and felt a rush of warmth and happiness flow through him.

This was it. He had found the answer to all of his after-school problems! Nothing could ruin his happiness now!

5

The next twenty-four hours flew by the way the scenery had on Shepard Lake Trail. Today Will had eaten lunch with Candy and Mitch. He could sense other kids wondering how he'd managed to get so tight with them so quickly.

The same thing had happened a couple of times when he'd passed Ace Diamond in the hall and the older boy had given him the special handshake. Every eye in the hall had been on Will then, and he liked it. He felt like one of the really popular kids for the first time in his life. It was a heady, wonderful feeling.

After school, Will made his way across the street to the town library. He figured he could get onto a mountain biking Web site or chat room on the Internet, or maybe look at some books about it.

But as he came into the big reading area, with its old wooden tables lined up one after the other, he saw Danny sitting there, doing his homework.

They hadn't talked all week. Since last Saturday, Will had just been too busy with his newfound hobby.

But Danny was still in the world of the lonely latchkey child, the brainiac who spent his afternoons studying alone. Will suddenly felt sorry for him. Danny would have loved mountain biking, too, if he ever tried it — Will was sure of that. But he wasn't so sure he could convince Danny. He plopped his book bag down on the table and sat down across from his old friend.

"Danny," he began, "how's it going?"

"Okay, I guess," Danny replied with a shrug. "Everybody's been talking about you today, you know."

"Really?" Will shifted in his seat. The idea that he was the subject of people's conversations made him a little uncomfortable. "What are they saying?"

"They're saying you're a poser and a wannabe. Some of them, anyway."

"Who?" Will wanted to know, hurt that anyone would think that way about him.

"Oh, no," Danny said, shaking his head. "I'm not gonna get into the middle of this. You asked me what people were saying." He peered at Will through his thick glasses. "A few people also said you were okay."

"Who! Who?" Will had to know.

Danny drummed his fingers on the table. "No one. I made the whole thing up," Danny said. "What do you care what people think, anyway?"

"You made the whole thing up?" Will repeated, stunned.

"Maybe yes, maybe no," Danny said cryptically. "So what is all this about, anyway? Are you 'acting out' or something?"

"What do you mean?" Will asked. "I don't get you."

"I mean," Danny said, rolling his eyes, "on Saturday afternoon the two of us are nearly killed by a marauding pack of maniacs on mountain bikes, and instead of fighting back or swearing revenge or at least being mildly annoyed, you go out and spend hundreds of dollars on a murder weapon of your own and join the Ace Diamond Fan Club. Does that strike you as weird, or is it just me?"

"Whew," Will said, blowing out a deep breath. "Jeez, Danny, chill out. I thought you would have gotten over it by now."

"Oh, okay, so *I'm* the one who's acting strangely." Danny's voice dripped with sarcasm. "I should have realized."

"Look," Will said, trying to get through to his friend, "it's just that I knew, when those bikes came flying down the trail — I knew I wanted to do that."

Danny seemed dumbstruck. "Really? Why?" This time, his voice was incredulous.

"It has to be the greatest feeling," Will said dreamily. "Total speed and freedom, nature — I don't know, everything!"

"You're not telling me you've already gone down a mountain," Danny said.

"No, not yet," Will admitted. "But —"

"Then you don't *know* anything," Danny insisted. "You're only imagining. And while you're doing it, imagine the terrified hikers you'll be passing on your way down. Imagine hitting one of them."

"Cut it out, Danny. You know I would never hit anybody."

"Well, either you would or you wouldn't," Danny insisted. "If you wouldn't, then quit thinking you're going to fly down the mountain. 'Cause you can't do that and be careful, too."

"I think you can." Will held his ground. "I'll bet I can."

Just then, the librarian came over to shush them, and they both opened their books and started doing homework.

Will's reverie was broken. Suddenly there was a downside to his new hobby. He hadn't realized just how upset Danny was about the incident on Saturday. Unless he could make Danny see how great mountain biking was, it might come between the two of them. Will might even wind up losing his best, oldest friend. And he sure didn't want that to happen.

On Friday at two-thirty the club met outside the gym doors. Everyone was in a great mood. There was no school the next day, and they had all weekend to do their homework. This afternoon was strictly for fun!

Will, like the rest of them, had left his book bag in his locker, knowing that the school would remain open all afternoon and evening, as it did every Friday.

He would retrieve his bag later. All he carried now were a few granola bars crammed into his pockets and his two trusty water bottles, which fit neatly into holders on the sides of his bike frame.

Even though he'd been in the club for only a few days, he felt totally at home with the other bikers. Everyone had welcomed him warmly from the first moment. Even Ace, who had some reason to be angry at Will for buying "his" bike, was being super-friendly. Will wondered why anyone would ever have a problem with Ace.

Following Gail's schedule, they rode out to Slide Mountain. The ski resort was a good eight miles out of town, and they had to be careful of traffic. But once they were there, they registered, paid the small entry fee, and got ready for their ride uphill.

"I hope you're ready for this, Will," Gail said. "It's

hard work. Just ride alongside me or just ahead of me. I'll give you some pointers if you're in trouble."

"Oh, don't worry about me," Will said confidently. "I'll be fine."

Famous last words. After five minutes of exhausting pedaling, Will had to stop to catch his breath. Gail called out for the others to meet at the trail head, then came back to check on Will.

"You okay?" she asked.

"Yeah," Will gasped. "But this is harder than I thought." He stared longingly up at the ski lift and noticed that plenty of riders had their bikes hanging on the lift as they rode comfortably to the top.

Gail noticed his longing look. "Forget it," she said. "We only use those when we go on the advanced trails. We're doing the bunny slope today."

"Oh."

"Are you sure you're okay?" she asked.

"Yeah," he assured her, his breath finally back to normal. "I don't know what the trouble is. Maybe I'm not shifting right or something."

"No, it isn't that," Gail said. "You're, like, not getting up and over the bike enough."

"Huh?"

"You have to lean more forward to keep your momentum going," she advised, demonstrating. "Go ahead — I'll follow you. Just remember to stay forward on the bike."

Will tried it, and sure enough, he was able to get the bike going and keep it going, all the way up to the trail head. Still, he was huffing and puffing by the time he made it. The others were waiting for him there, applauding him as he pedaled the last few yards.

Will flushed with embarrassment. He *stunk* at mountain biking!

"Hey, don't feel bad," Candy said, smiling. "It's hard going uphill."

"Yeah, tell me about it!" Will said, managing a laugh. "Now I know why there aren't a hundred kids in this club."

"Hey, don't knock mountain biking," Ace warned him sternly. "It isn't for everybody. That's just the point. Who wants a huge crowd on the trail, anyway? Not me!" He clapped Will on the shoulder. "You got up here okay," he told him. "Not bad for a first time. Proud of you, kid."

Will grinned from ear to ear. "Thanks," he said, feeling a lump of pride in his throat. Looking out at the snowcapped mountains in the distance and feeling the fresh wind in his face, Will took a moment to bask in the new friendships he'd made.

Will took a few long drinks of water and ate a granola bar. After a few minutes, Gail checked her watch, looked at the sun getting lower in the sky, and said, "Okay, guys. It's time to go down!"

"Ya-hoo!" Ace and Steven yelled. "Ya-hooooooo!"

The sound chilled Will. That yell was identical to the one he and Danny had heard from the maniac bikers on the mountain. He looked at Ace and Steven and wondered if it were possible. . . .

"Let's go!" Mitch called. "Come on, Will!"

"Just remember to feather your brakes," Gail reminded him. "It will help you keep an even pace. And use your feet to steady you whenever you have any sense of trouble."

"Okay," Will said, nodding and concentrating as he shoved off.

"Above all, watch out for hikers, horses, et cetera," Gail called out to him. "You never know who's out there, and we sure don't want anybody getting hurt."

They went single file, spaced out at safe intervals, so they wouldn't risk collisions. There were boulders, and tree roots, and dips in the terrain to watch out for. Will found himself applying the brakes a lot. It wasn't scary, but he wasn't ready to go too fast — not on his first downhill run.

Far ahead, he could hear Ace and Steve, and the others, too, whooping it up as they careened down the trail. But Will didn't try to catch up with them. He found himself being ultra-careful, and it surprised him. Dimly he wondered if it could have anything to do with the near-accident he and Danny had had.

At first, most of Will's attention was focused on staying on the bike and not falling. He bounced over rocks and ruts, felt the jarring sensations shoot up his arms. His leg muscles burned with the effort of keeping his pace steady.

Gradually he grew more confident. He realized that if he let his arms go limp instead of holding them stiff, they'd absorb the shocks better. He feathered his brakes less often and let his pace increase. Finally he became aware of the wind rushing up at him and the trees whooshing by on either side. The sensation of full flight was totally awesome!

It was heart-pounding, second-splitting action, all right. It was about the most exciting thing he'd ever done! As he neared the bottom, he could see that they were all waiting for him, cheering him on, waving and laughing.

Once again, though, they were laughing *with* him, not *at* him. "Hey, you made it!" Ace shouted, applauding and whistling. "Whoo-hoo!"

"Yeah, Will!" Steve Barrad shouted, giving Will the mountain biker's handshake. Mitch and the others followed suit, giving Will multiple slaps on the back till he cried out for mercy.

It was only on the way back to town that Will thought about Danny again. Ace, riding beside him, noticed the look on his face. "What's up, kid?" he asked. "Something bothering you?"

"Nah, not really," Will said.

"Don't jive me," Ace said, looking him right in the

eyes as they rode side by side. "What's going on? Tell me."

Will sighed. "It's my best friend, Danny. He hates mountain biking. I wish I could get him to try it."

"He hates mountain biking?" Ace repeated. "Will, forget about him, man. Just dump him. He's a loser."

"He's not a loser," Will protested, startled by Ace's curt dismissal of Danny.

"Whatever," Ace responded, clearly unconvinced. "Tell me one thing. Has he ever tried it? Huh? Has he ever even been on a mountain bike?"

"I don't think so," Will had to admit.

"I rest my case," Ace said. "Do what you want, but I'll tell you, if it were me, I wouldn't bother with anyone who doesn't like mountain biking. Mountain biking, that's what I'm all about. You don't like it, you don't like me." He looked sideways at Will. "And I got a feeling mountain biking is gonna be you, too. Am I right?"

Will nodded. "Yeah," he said, looking ahead at the road. "Yeah, I guess so."

But inside, Will knew he didn't mean it. He liked

mountain biking a lot — even loved it — but it wasn't "what he was all about."

If only he could find a way to get Danny interested in the club! But he knew it was impossible.

Glancing over at Ace, he felt certain that Danny and Ace would never hit it off. Not in a million years.

6

That night, Will didn't sleep well. He kept dreaming he was on his mountain bike, going down a sloping trail at full speed. Suddenly there stood Danny, right in front of him! Danny opened his mouth to scream, but nothing came out. Instead, from behind him, Will heard a maniacal voice yelling, "Ya-hoo!" He woke up in a cold sweat, his heart pounding.

On Saturday morning, he called Danny first thing and invited him to go hiking again. But Danny wasn't exactly overjoyed to hear from him.

"I thought you'd be out mountain biking with your new pals," he said.

"Hey, new friends are great, but old friends are greater," Will assured him.

"Yeah, well . . ." Danny's voice trailed off.

"So, how about it? Should we get a good hike in?" Will asked.

"I don't think so," Danny said. "I don't really feel like it today. You go ahead, though."

"I can't go by myself," Will said sourly. "You sure?"

"Yeah," Danny said. "I don't know why. I guess nearly getting killed last week, then having you turn into one of the killers, turned me off to it."

"Oh, come off it, Danny," Will said in frustration. "It wasn't that close. We got out of the way okay, didn't we?"

"Just barely," Danny said. "Hiking's not what it used to be. Not since the mountain bikers took over the trails."

This was going nowhere, Will could tell. "Okay, see ya," he said, and hung up quickly. Danny's rejection had stung him badly. What had he done to deserve that?

Sure, he'd taken up mountain biking. If Danny was really his friend, he'd be happy for him! And so what if Will had made friends with the kids in the club? It was only natural, wasn't it, to be friends with people you had things in common with?

Well, if Danny didn't want to be his friend, that was his tough luck, Will decided. He hadn't done anything to offend him, and if Danny was going to be like that, let him.

Will got dressed and went downstairs to the kitchen, where his parents were eating breakfast.

"Hi, sleepyhead!" his mom greeted him. "It's nine o'clock already. We decided to eat without you!"

"It's okay," Will assured her, plopping down into a chair.

"What's up with you today, son?" his dad asked, putting down his newspaper.

"Nothing much," Will said with a shrug. "Could we go to the mall? I could use some biking shorts and a shirt or two."

"Uh-oh, here we go," his dad said. "The money pit —"

"Bob," Will's mom interrupted. "We haven't spent any time with Will all week. I think going to the mall might be a nice idea."

Just then, the doorbell rang, and the conversation halted while Will ran to get it.

He threw the door open, and there was Ace Diamond, his bike parked behind him on the walk.

"Hey, kid," he said. "Mitch told me where you lived. You want to go for a ride or something?"

"Me?" Will asked, not quite believing that Ace Diamond — *the* Ace Diamond! — was standing on his doorstep.

"You see anybody else around here?" Ace asked comically. "Yeah, you. I'm riding the coolest trail today, and I thought I'd show you what mountain biking's really all about."

"Excellent!" Will said, giving Ace the handshake. Then he ran back inside to tell his parents to forget about the mall. He was going riding!

His parents, though bewildered at his sudden change in energy and attitude, quickly gave their permission. They were sorry not to have the time with Will but thrilled that he was so excited about what he was doing.

And so, five minutes later, Will and Ace were heading down one of the two-lane blacktop roads leading out of town into the neighboring hills. Montwood was surrounded by hills on three sides, and on the fourth, a sloping plateau led down toward the west. There, Shepard Lake and several others nestled against the slopes of the Coast Range. Beyond those forested mountains lay the Pacific Ocean, forty miles away.

Everywhere you rode around Montwood, Will was discovering, there were dirt roads and mountain trails to bike on.

"Wait till you see where we're going!" Ace called out to him over his shoulder. As always, when they were on paved roads, they went single file. Still, whenever a long straightaway showed that there was no traffic coming, Ace would drop back to talk with him.

"It's right up ahead," Ace told him, after they'd been pedaling hard, mostly uphill, for about fifteen minutes. "Right . . . here!"

In a flash, Ace peeled off the road onto a bumpy, narrow trail leading right through the woods. Will braked hard and nearly went over as he swerved onto the path and bounced over the ditch that cut through it. "Yikes!" he yelled. "Hey, wait for me!"

Ace was off and riding now, taking air whenever an obstacle presented itself, as the trail wound up, down, up, and down again, like a BMX racecourse.

"Ya-hoo!" Ace let out his trademark yell. After a moment's hesitation, Will imitated it, trying like anything to keep up his speed and still not lose his balance.

"Follow me — we're goin' down!" Ace shouted, and dipped down with the trail, suddenly disappearing from sight. Behind him, he threw something small that glinted in the sun. Will passed it, and saw that it was a gum wrapper.

Will was shocked that Ace would just litter the trail like that, but he had no time to think about it. The trail dove steeply downward, and Will went with it, his feet down on the ground to steady and slow the suddenly careening bike. "Yaaah!" he yelled, paralyzed with fear as he struggled to control his bike.

Ahead of him, Will saw Ace leap into the air with his bike, coming down ten feet later on the other side of a huge mud puddle.

"Aaaahhh!" Will tried to brake, and when he saw that it was too late, he made a feeble attempt to jump the puddle. He came down smack in the middle of it!

The next thing he heard was Ace's roaring laughter. "Yeah! All right! You're initiated, kid! Mudface, that's you!"

He gave Will the club handshake, and Will, who had been steaming with anger only a moment before, suddenly decided he didn't want Ace to know how scared he'd been.

"So, what do you think of it?" Ace asked. "This place rules, doesn't it?"

"It's amazing," Will said, not wanting to disagree. The trail had been fun but far too dangerous for a beginner like him, with its boulders and steep pitch, its roots and crevices and deep mud holes. He was surprised Ace had taken him here, knowing Will had been riding less than a week. "Does the club ever come here?"

"Are you kidding?" Ace asked with a snort. "They would never come to a place like this! They're attached to the school, right? So they have to worry about insurance and stuff, like if somebody got hurt and sued."

"Yeah, I can see how they might worry about that," Will agreed.

"It wasn't too much for you, was it?" Ace asked slyly.

71

Will quickly shook his head. "Me? Nah."

"Great!" Ace said, grinning broadly. "A mountain biker is born! Let's do it again!"

Will had felt the thrill of it, for sure, but he'd also been scared stiff — this trail was far too advanced for him, and he knew it. "Uh, actually," Will said, "I should be getting back. I'm supposed to go to the mall with my folks later."

"Okay," Ace said. "I'll see you Monday."

"You're not going back?" Will asked, surprised.

"Nah, what for?" Ace asked. "If I show up at the bike store, my dad will just put me to work. It's my weekend, you know? I'd rather hang out here, even if it is by myself."

"What about Steve and Mitch? How come you didn't ask them to come?" Will asked.

"Them? Mitch's parents make him and his sister go to their country house every weekend, and Steve used to come, but lately, his folks . . ." His voice trailed off.

"What?" Will asked.

Ace frowned. "They don't like for their baby to ride with the big bad wolf, here," he said, pointing to himself. "They think I'm gonna get little Stevie in trouble."

"Are you?" Will asked, jokingly, but curious about the answer.

"You're still in one piece, aren't you?" Ace asked.

"Yeah." Barely, he added silently.

"You had fun, right?"

"Yeah," Will said again, only with less certainty.

"So okay," Ace concluded. "See? Nothing to worry about. See you Monday, huh?"

"Sure thing," Will said, and kicked off down the dirt track that led toward the main road. "See you."

As he pedaled, Will thought again about the gum wrapper Ace had deliberately dropped on the trail. Such a small thing, really. And yet, more than Ace's poor judgment in taking Will to a trail that was way too advanced for him, it was the gum wrapper that, for some strange reason, seemed to stick in Will's mind.

On Monday it rained hard all day, and when Will checked at the gym doors at two-thirty, none of the club members was there. He figured the meeting was canceled and just went home. So he was surprised that night when Gail Chen called and asked where he'd been.

"We were meeting in the gym office," she told him. "That's where we go when the weather's just too bad. Sorry, I should have told you that."

"It's okay," Will said. "Next time I'll know. Hey, where are we going on Wednesday?"

"To the South Fork Reservation," Gail said. "There are lots of nice trails there. Not too hilly, in case it's still soggy from today."

"Why, what happens when it's soggy?" Will asked. "I thought getting dirty was part of the fun."

"Yeah, up to a point," Gail agreed with a giggle. "But the trails get bad ruts if you skid on them while they're wet. Then the ruts harden as they dry, and the trail gets really messed up."

"I see," Will said, thinking of the muddy trail Ace had taken him to. The two of them had dug some ruts for sure. Will almost mentioned it, but something made him hold back. "Well, sorry I missed you today, anyway," he said. "See you Wednesday."

Will hung up and stared out his window at the rain, still coming down hard on the windowpane.

He had already eaten dinner and done his homework, so he took out the book he'd gotten from the library — a novel about mountain biking, where this bunch of kids gets stranded on a wilderness ride.

Funny, but ever since he'd started it, Will had begun to feel differently about reading. He was actually looking forward to tomorrow afternoon, sitting at the big library table, reading chapter after chapter of his book.

He was changing so fast that he barely recognized himself!

Across the library table sat Danny, a large volume of the Encyclopedia Brittanica spread out before him. He was copying notes from one of the pages.

Will peeked up from his novel every once in a while to glance at him. Finally his curiosity overwhelmed him. "What are you studying up on?" he asked.

"The ancient city of Ur," Danny replied. "It was in the Fertile Crescent, between the Tigris and Euphrates Rivers, where modern-day Iraq is."

"Oh. Iraq," Will said, nodding, but not really

getting why Danny was so interested in it. "Are you doing a report on it or something?"

"No," Danny said with a shrug. "It's just interesting — that's all."

"Uh-huh," Will said noncommittally. That was Danny. He just liked to learn about things, for the sake of knowing. Well, Will guessed he wasn't so different. Here he was, reading about mountain biking, and he didn't have any homework on it, either.

Just then, the library door burst open, and Ace Diamond marched in. He went up to the librarian and asked for something he had written down on a scrap of paper. He handed it to the librarian, and she went off to find whatever it was.

Meanwhile, Ace looked around and saw Will and Danny. Grinning mischievously, he came over to them. "Hey, kid!" he said, too loudly for the library. "So this is where you've been hiding! Just can't stay away from the books, huh?"

"I have to stay here on Tuesdays and Thursdays after school," Will explained. "It's part of my agreement with my parents, in exchange for them getting me the bike and letting me be in the club."

"Letting you?" Ace said, wincing. "Oh, gee, I forgot you were in sixth grade. But couldn't you just be home alone? I do it all the time."

"You do?" Will asked as Danny looked silently on.

"Sure. My mom and dad both work in the cycle shop. So I would have to work, too, if I showed up there. Forget that. I just go hang out downtown with some kids at the video arcade and the pizza place. You could come with us sometime if you wanted to chill with us."

"Sure!" Will said, then felt a sudden stab of guilt, as if he were betraying Danny or something, although of course, that was ridiculous. He wasn't doing that, was he?

Ace jerked his chin at Danny. "Is this the friend of yours who can't stand mountain biking?" he asked.

Will went beet red. Now Danny would know Will had been talking about him with his new friends! Will could feel Danny's hurt gaze on him without even looking at him.

"Yeah, that's me," Danny said. "I almost got killed by a couple of mountain bikers recently. So did Will, but it seems not to be bothering him any."

"That's because Will's got guts," Ace said, leaning

77

over the table. "Mountain biking is da bomb. You should try it sometime."

"Yeah, right. That'll be the day," Danny said, slamming his book shut.

"Loser," Ace said. "Don't reject what you don't know anything about!"

Will sat there, mortified, wanting to jump to Danny's defense, yet not wanting to get on Ace's bad side, either. The silence seemed to drag on indefinitely.

Just then, the librarian called to Ace. She had his book apparently, and he left to retrieve it. "So long, kid," he said to Will. And then he gave a half-smile and added, "So long, loser!"

When Ace had left, Will turned around to find Danny staring at him, white with rage. "Danny," he said, "I —"

"Never mind," Danny stopped him. "I don't want to hear it."

"Okay, I guess," Will said sheepishly. "But — are we still friends?"

"Friends?" Danny choked. "Friends stick up for each other, don't they, Will?"

He didn't wait for an answer. Instead, still shaking

with fury, he walked right past Will and out the library door.

Will bit his lip. He felt like sinking into the floor. He would have given anything to rewind and do over the last five minutes.

But what would he have done differently? Stick up for Danny and lose his friendship with Ace? He wasn't prepared to do that.

And what about your friendship with Danny? a little voice inside him asked.

Will didn't have an answer. He picked up his book and tried to concentrate on the words instead.

7

The next morning, Will rode the seven blocks to school just as he always did. But when he pedaled onto the school campus and locked up his bike on the rack next to the athletic field, he had the strangest feeling that someone was watching him. He turned around quickly and caught two separate groups of people huddled together, whispering and staring in his direction. One kid was even pointing at him.

What was going on? Will wasn't bold enough to go right up to the kids and ask them, but as he went inside by the main entrance, he saw a large knot of students gathered around a small table that had been set up in the hallway. Will stood patiently at the back of the crowd, waiting for a chance to get close enough to see what it was all about.

"Are you going to sign it?" one girl was asking another. "Sure, why not? The guy at the table sounds like he almost got creamed by one of them."

Just then one of the girls caught Will looking at them and fell silent. Others in the crowd did, too. Will had a sudden premonition that somehow mountain biking was involved with all the commotion. He jostled his way to the front of the line.

Sure enough, spread out on the table was a petition with the heading *Citizens Against Mountain Biking*. A handwritten sign behind it read *Stop abuses by mountain bikers! Sign to protect citizens' safety!*

Will read the petition in disbelief:

It has come to our attention that mountain bikers are often rude, careless, and dangerous in their use of public paths and trails. They make a lot of noise and litter; scare animals, old people, and children; ruin paths; and endanger the lives of everyone else using these public areas. Therefore, we, the undersigned, hereby demand that mountain bikes be banned from all hiking and riding trails, ski trails, and any other unpaved roads on public lands around town.

Furthermore, so that Hopgood Middle School not be seen as encouraging this dangerous and environmentally disastrous sport, we demand that this school's mountain biking club be disbanded at once.

Underneath, there were pages and pages of lines for people to sign on. So far, two of the pages were full.

Will stood there staring at it in utter dismay. Even though there was a girl sitting behind the table, Will knew without a doubt that Danny had to be behind this fiasco. He recognized his friend's writing style. And to think, just the day before, he'd been feeling sorry about how he'd treated Danny!

The traitor! It was one thing for him to be angry and another for him to try to spoil everyone else's fun! Will felt like taking the petition and ripping it to shreds, but there were lots of kids behind him still waiting to read it. He moved off toward his locker, still steaming, and wracking his brain to figure out a way to save the club.

Will had always known that there were some people who didn't like mountain bikes or the people who rode them. But he had thought they were just a few cranks, or maybe people who'd been personally affected, like Danny. But he was totally floored by how many people were lining up to sign the petition.

They just don't understand how great mountain biking is! he thought miserably. If only he and the others could show them — maybe make a home video and show it, or give a talk, or — no, that wouldn't work. The feeling you got when you were riding the trail couldn't be put into words, unless you were a good writer like Danny — and Danny was leading the other side!

Will felt like punching Danny, but he knew he wouldn't do it. How could he have felt sorry for that jerk?

He was still steaming when Ace collared him in the lunch line later that day. "I've been looking for you all over!" Ace said, pulling Will by the shirt. "Come on, I've got everybody together out back."

He led Will outside through a set of side doors to the bike racks, where all the other members of the club were already waiting. "Okay, everybody's here," Ace said. "I guess you all know why I got us together."

Gail looked uncomfortable. "I don't understand how this happened," she said. "We haven't done anything to offend anybody."

"Of course we haven't!" Ace agreed. Will had a momentary flash of Ace dissing Danny in the library, but he didn't say anything. Ace was obviously mad, and he wasn't the kind of guy you wanted angry at you.

"I say we strike back!" Ace was saying as he paced back and forth in front of them. "We could find out who wrote it and trash their locker!"

"Yeah!" Mitch and Steve both chimed in.

"I don't know," Candy said, biting her lip. "That sounds kind of extreme."

"Yeah," Juliette agreed. "We don't want to prove them right, whatever we do."

"Absolutely!" Gail agreed.

"Hey, we're not taking this lying down, no matter what you say!" Ace told Gail, shaking a finger in her face. "All right, look — tomorrow, everyone be here half an hour before school, on your bikes, with whatever you can find that will make a lot of noise. Make up some slogans to chant, and tell everyone you know who bikes to come, too. We want to show strength in numbers."

"Hey," Gail protested, as the other members of the club all nodded in agreement with Ace's proposal. "Wait a minute. I'm the president of the club, and if we're going to do something like that, we have to have a vote!"

Ace scowled and shook his head. "The vote's already been taken, in case you haven't noticed," he told her. "Be there." Having silenced Gail, Ace turned to the others and grinned nastily. "Okay, everybody, no ride this afternoon. Go home and get your stuff together. Tomorrow," he said, "is Biker Pride Day."

The next day was Thursday. It was a beautiful, sunny, early October day, and at recess, everyone in the whole school headed out onto the school campus to enjoy the weather.

What greeted them there was a circling group of about two dozen mountain bikers, in full gear, blowing on noisemakers and chanting slogans at the top of their lungs.

"Biking beats hiking! Biking beats hiking!"

"Be like Mike! Get on a bike!"

"Bikers have rights, too!"

"Stay out of our way, and we'll stay out of yours!"

Ace led the cheers and made sure all the others yelled as loudly as he did. Not all of them were in the club — most had been drafted by club members to beef up the ranks. But all of them followed Ace's directions. As Will had learned, Ace was the kind of person who, when he said to do something, you didn't argue. You just did it.

Only Gail did not join in the chanting. In fact, after a minute or two, she stopped riding in the circle, too. "This is totally stupid," she said, taking off her helmet and shaking her head in disgust. "We're just making a spectacle of ourselves. I'm outta here." She walked her bike away.

"Ignore her," Ace ordered the rest of them. "She's just bugged because I thought of this idea, not her. But who needs her?"

He started another chant. By this time, a crowd of onlookers had gathered. Most of them just laughed or shook their heads. Some applauded the bikers and cheered them on. Will wondered if they really meant it or if they were just having a good time at the bikers' expense.

He realized that he sort of felt the way Gail did. All this attention made him very uncomfortable, and he was afraid the club might get in trouble for it. Worse, he could sense that they were just turning more people against them with their annoying tactics.

Still, Will figured, he was in it this far, and he might as well go with it all the way. He opened his mouth and chanted along with the others, trying to ignore his sense of impending doom.

The protest was the talk of the school all afternoon. When classes let out, Will got his book bag and started off to the library as usual. Then something stopped him in his tracks. It was the image of Danny's face in his mind. Danny, who would surely be sitting there at his usual table, doing his homework or studying up on something he was interested in. Danny, who obviously hated his guts by now.

Will retreated back onto the sidewalk. No, he didn't have the nerve, or the desire, to face Danny. Not right now. Not today.

Instead, he headed over to the bike racks. Maybe he'd take a little ride around town himself, just for the fun of it. He knew better than to head for woodland trails on his own, but on-road biking was another matter.

As he walked over, he spotted Ace talking to Candy and Mitch. The twins looked upset.

"Hey, Will!" Mitch called out. "Guess what?"

"What?" Will asked.

"The principal read the petition, saw our demonstration, and decided to review the club's status," Ace explained calmly. "No meetings until further notice."

"What?" Will gasped. "That stinks!"

"Ace says it isn't really that bad," Candy said.

Ace jumped in to explain. "It just means Mr. Rivera's listening to both sides. Once he looks at the facts, he'll let us ride, and then there won't be any more petitions."

When nobody responded, Ace went on. "We sure got his attention!" he said, nodding in satisfaction. "We showed him there are two sides to the story."

"I don't know . . . ," Will said, shaking his head. He didn't finish, but inside, he was thinking, If the principal was so impressed with their protest, why was he suspending the club until further notice?

"Come on," Ace said. "I say we just go riding. So what if we can't have a club? They can't stop us from biking!"

"Yeah!" Mitch agreed.

"Wait, though," Candy said. "We have to go home, Mitch. We're going to the dentist, remember?"

"Oh, yeah. Right. Oh, well, see you tomorrow," Mitch told Ace and Will. "Or whenever we get to meet again, that is."

He and Candy biked away, waving good-bye. Ace turned to Will. "Wanna go ride someplace?" he asked with a mischievous grin.

"I'm supposed to stay at the library this afternoon," Will said truthfully.

"You know," Ace said, making a face, "that is the dumbest deal I have ever heard of. I mean, what do your folks think, that you're going to magically fall in love with reading all of a sudden if they force you to go to the library? That is so lame!"

"Yeah," Will said, just to avoid talking about it. He didn't want to tell Ace he was reading his third book in the past two weeks. In fact, ever since he'd been hanging out at the library, Will had been reading every night for at least half an hour before bed. His grades had improved a bit, too. Getting a head start on his homework didn't hurt, and neither did the extra studying he'd started doing.

"You wouldn't catch me in there unless I absolutely *had* to be. I wouldn't care what my parents said." Ace snorted in disgust. "Look, let's just go for a ride, huh? Just you and me. The two latchkey kids. Rebels, that's us! Come on. Your parents don't have to know."

"Okay . . . I guess . . . ," Will agreed tentatively. "As long as I'm back home by six."

"Sure, I'll get you back by then," Ace said, strapping on his helmet. "Hey, I've never shown you the ramps! Follow me!"

"The ramps? What are they?" Will called after him, hopping on his bike and taking off in pursuit.

Ace headed straight for Brookfield Park. It was a big county park, with ball fields, tennis courts, playgrounds, and wooded areas with picnic tables and horse trails. Ace sped straight down the paved pedestrian paths. He slowed at one point, pulled something out of his backpack, and launched it into a garbage can. Will passed the same can a moment later, and tried to see what it was Ace had thrown out. But he only caught a glimpse of red and something that looked like a can.

Musta been soda pop or a sport drink, Will figured as he pedaled harder to try to catch up with the speedy Ace.

"Beep! Beep!" Ace called out.

Ace shot past two startled mothers, who whisked their toddlers out of harm's way. When Will rode by a moment later, they yelled some nasty things at him.

Will barely had time to say "Sorry!" to the women, because Ace was already racing toward the wooded part of the park, and Will didn't want to lose sight of him.

Will felt a prickle of annoyance at Ace. Why did he have to do the things he did? If he hadn't made such a fuss about "Biker Pride Day," the petition thing probably would have just blown over. And why did he have to litter and scare walkers? It was people like Ace who gave mountain biking a bad reputation, Will was beginning to realize.

Still, Ace had clearly accepted Will as his new,

close friend. And Ace was popular. Will didn't feel like he could afford to refuse that friendship. If he did, he could kiss his new status at school good-bye. And besides, now that Danny, his ex–best friend, hated his guts, Will didn't have anyone to hang out with. Since joining the bike club, he hadn't spent much time with his few other pals. If he made Ace angry at him, too, he was sure he'd lose all his friends in the club. Then where would he be? In a social loser land — that's where.

Ace led him to a path that was hidden from the rest of the park by low-hanging branches of the surrounding trees. Here, a series of natural ramps had been worn into the ground by mountain bikers over the years. There were bumps, jumps, ruts, and dangerous turns — a great practice course!

"Follow me!" Ace told him. "And watch out for the first turn — it's a killer!" Ace took the ramp at full speed, and Will followed at a more cautious pace.

The ramp was really fun — just hard enough to provide some good thrills without actually endangering your health. It was the kind of place where you could become a really good mountain biker without risk of running into nonbikers. Right now, that was important to Will.

After about twenty minutes, the two boys paused to drink some water and catch their breath.

"Great place!" Will commented truthfully. "It's cool to have a spot just for mountain bikers."

Ace shook his head. "Mountain bikers can go anywhere, kiddo — that's what these babies are built for!" He patted his bike.

"Yeah, but Ace, you nearly killed those ladies and their kids back there. You really ought to watch out."

"Get real," Ace said, scowling. "Those people ought to pay attention to the world around them. It's like, wake up!" He laughed, then took a long gulp of water.

"Yeah, but that's what gets people mad at bikers," Will said, trying not to sound argumentative.

But Ace's mind was on something else. "Do you realize," he said, "that those mothers do not go to work? There they are, spending their whole entire day with their kids. All day, every day."

"Yeah, well, those kids are little," Will pointed out.

"My mom went back to work eight weeks after I was born," Ace said grimly. "My real mother was the TV."

Will swallowed hard, not sure how to react. "My mom just went back to work full-time last summer," he ventured. "I watched a lot of TV, too, for a while. Till I started mountain biking."

Ace emptied his water bottle slowly onto the ground. "I'm telling you, if your mother really cared about you, she wouldn't work full-time. It's totally selfish."

"Well —"

"It's all about 'me, me, me and how much money can I make,' right?" Ace demanded.

"I guess —"

"Do your parents really need all that money?" Ace asked. "Tell the truth. I mean, you're the one who told me your dad works till eight at night."

"Seven, actually," Will corrected him.

"Seven, eight, whatever." Ace waved him off. "And he drives a nice car, right? And look at the house you live in. Your parents have plenty of money, but your mom would rather work than be

94

with you." He poked a finger at Will's bike. "And to top it all off, they were too cheap to spend some of that dough on new goods for you." He shook his head. "Take it from me, kid. It's pure selfishness."

Will didn't say anything. Part of him felt like sticking up for his mom. Yet another, angry part of him suddenly realized that what Ace was saying was something he himself had been feeling for months. It came as a big shock to Will to realize that he had such feelings. But he knew it was true, and the knowledge left him feeling hollow.

They rode some more, but Will's heart wasn't in it. He mostly kept silent, thinking back again and again to the day in June when his mom had first told him about her new job. And he felt his anger rising inside him, like a great, hot, black blob that had been kept down too long.

Will checked his watch. Dang! He was late for dinner. And he still had to stop at school to pick up his backpack. His mother was going to be mad. She knew the library closed at five-thirty. It was already six-thirty. She was going to let him have it, all right.

Well, so what if she's mad? Will asked himself.

He was mad, too! He was madder than her, and had been for a long time. She and his father didn't care about him. So why should he obey their rules? And if they wanted to fight about it, that was fine with him!

8

By the time Will came home, he was steaming mad. He came in, slammed the door behind him, and dropped his backpack right there in the front hall, where he knew he wasn't supposed to leave it.

He could hear his mom in the kitchen, taking out plates to set the table. Even from here, he could smell the Chinese food. He remembered when she used to cook meals, back before she went to work full-time. It seemed like years ago. The good old days.

"Will? Is that you?" she called. When he didn't answer, she repeated, "Will? Come in here, please. I want to talk with you about something."

Great. Just great. Now what? Was she going to tell him she was working late at the office all next month? He shuffled off to the kitchen with a big chip on his shoulder.

"Yeah? What is it?" he asked in a sour tone of voice as he entered the room and sat down on one of the breakfast stools.

What she said took him totally by surprise. "I just got a call from Mr. Rivera," she said. "He said you were involved in some trouble today. Do you want to tell me about it?"

Will couldn't believe it! If the principal had called his house, he must also have called the houses of all the other club members. This was not good news. It meant that Mr. Rivera felt they had done something really bad.

"What did he say?" Will asked.

"Never mind that," his mother said. "I want your version first."

"Well," Will began, shifting uncomfortably in his chair, "these other kids were having a petition to ban mountain biking around Montwood and disband the mountain biking club, so we all thought we'd fight back."

"By disrupting the school recess and vandalizing the school?" she asked, looking dismayed. "Will, I thought you had better sense than to get involved in this kind of thing!"

"But Mom, all we did was make noise and chant slogans and sort of ride around the basketball courts so kids couldn't just play and ignore us."

"And spray graffiti on the school walls?" his mother added pointedly.

"What? We did not! That's a lie!"

"Well, someone did," she shot back. "Someone sprayed 'Mountain Bike Mania,' in big red letters. It's going to cost the school quite a bit to get it cleaned, too. Mr. Rivera warned me that if you were found to have done it, or even knew about it, you'd be suspended. So I want the truth, and I want it now."

She sat there across from him, her arms crossed. Will found himself fuming. "I didn't do it, Mom, and neither did any of the others!" he said hotly. Almost as soon as the words were out of his mouth, though, the image of the object Ace had tossed into the garbage can came back to him. Could it have been a can of spray paint? Will wouldn't have put it past Ace to have snuck outside during lunch period to spray the message.

"All right," his mother said. "But I don't want you going off on your mountain bike until this whole thing has been settled."

"What?!"

"Look, I can see that you've been out biking this afternoon. And don't try to tell me you haven't. I can tell by the dirt on your shoes."

"Okay, so I did. I didn't feel like going to the library today."

"Oh, you didn't feel like it? What about your agreement with us? Doesn't that mean anything to you?"

Will gave a shrug.

"I suppose you've already heard that your biking club is under temporary suspension."

"No, duh," Will said, rolling his eyes.

"Will Matthews! Are you mocking me?" his mother asked incredulously. "What's gotten into you, young man?"

"Nothing," Will said, getting up off the stool to get away from her. He felt like she could see right through him, and he didn't want her to. "I'm just sticking up for myself, that's all. Just like you and Dad always do."

"What do you mean by that?" his mom asked. "And please turn around and look at me when we talk."

Will turned around, sighing deeply. "I mean, you wanted to make more money, even though we're not poor, so you went and got a job, even though we have to eat Chinese food every single night now. But that's okay, because it made you happy. Well, what about me? I finally found something that makes me happy, and now you won't let me do it!"

"Will, of course I want you to be happy!" she protested. "But I also expect you to act like a responsible person. If you expect to be allowed to go off mountain biking, you've got to abide by your agreements and stay out of trouble!" Her lower lip began to tremble. "And I'm sorry if I've been selfish, but having a career happens to mean a lot to me."

Will was torn between his anger and the shame he felt at upsetting his mother. He stormed out of the room, ran up the stairs, and slammed his bedroom door behind him. Collapsing onto the bed, he felt hot tears sting his cheeks.

His life was a total wreck! His best friend hated him, the principal thought he was a juvenile delinquent, he'd driven his own mother to near tears, and worst of all, his parents were never going to let him go mountain biking again!

Will and his parents didn't talk much for the next couple of days. A few times, Will was about to apologize, but just as he was about to say he was sorry, his dad or his mom would say something to get him all angry again. The family barely managed to have meals together, and the tension was so thick you could cut it with a knife.

The worst time was Friday after school. With no biking club, there was nothing to do except read and watch TV. Will didn't feel like reading today — it was something his parents would have approved of — so he just watched TV nonstop, before dinner and after, until he fell asleep in front of the tube around midnight.

The next morning, he had just eaten breakfast and was about to go flip on the TV again, when he saw Ace Diamond outside the kitchen window, signaling for Will to meet him outside.

Will's dad's face was hidden behind his newspaper. His mom was flipping through a magazine, eating her cereal. Neither one of them made any move to talk to him. What were they doing? he wondered. Waiting for him to make the first move? And they accused *him* of being immature!

Well, if he was angry, that was his business. He nodded through the window at Ace, then signaled for him to come around to the front of the house.

Will went into the living room and quietly opened the front door. "Hi," he said.

"Hey, I'm going riding," Ace said. "Wanna come?"

"Can't. I'm grounded, at least on my bike. Want to come in for a while?"

"Nah." Ace glanced around. "I can't believe this. Nobody's parents are letting them bike! It's all because Mr. Rivera called people's houses." Ace made a bitter face. "I hate that guy."

"Hey, Ace," Will asked, coming outside and closing the door behind him. "Do you know anything about some graffiti that got sprayed on the school walls?"

"Huh? Oh, that. No. What about it?"

Something in Ace's reaction told Will he knew more than he was telling, but Will let it pass. He figured it was pointless to argue with Ace Diamond.

Ace wasn't the kind of person you could convince of anything, and if you didn't watch yourself, before you knew it, he'd have convinced you of *his* point of view.

"Come on," Ace said. "My folks don't know I'm out either. I'm supposed to show up at the shop at ten."

"Won't they notice you're not there?" Will wondered.

"You think they care?" Ace retorted. "You think your parents care? You think they'll even notice you're gone?"

Will thought about it. His mom and dad would probably think he was up in his room on the computer. "Maybe not," he admitted.

"There, what did I tell you? Nobody really cares what we do. Come on, let's go. I've saved my favorite ride for today. We're gonna go for the gold, kid!"

Will nodded and opened the door a bit to see if his parents had noticed him go out. Nothing had changed. He shut the door again. "How far is this place?" he asked.

"In Morton State Forest," Ace told him. "The

canyon trail. It's da bomb, I'm telling you. Better than the best roller coaster!"

"Okay!" Will said in a whisper. The thrill of sneaking off and doing something forbidden crept over him. This would show his parents he couldn't be locked up in the house like some six-year-old!

The garage door was open. He got his bike and gear and backed out into the driveway. There, he straddled his bike while he put on his pads, gloves, and helmet. "I sure hope I don't get in trouble for this," he couldn't help saying as he gave his house one last backward glance.

"You're already in trouble," Ace shot back with a grin. "What's a little more gonna matter?"

All the way there — and it must have been a good seventeen miles — Ace talked to Will and Will listened. All about trails he'd ridden, and dares he'd taken, and bikes he'd tried, and maneuvers he'd perfected.

It seemed to Will that Ace knew everything there was to know about mountain biking. And hadn't Julian at the bike shop said so? Will soaked in the information, storing it away for future use.

At last, they arrived at the trail into the forest. Will checked his watch. They'd been gone just about an hour. With the ride, and the trip back, his parents were sure to notice that he was missing. What would they think? And what would they say when they learned the truth?

Will tried to put the thought out of his mind. The state forest was a fantastic place, with giant old trees soaring hundreds of feet into the air. There was very little undergrowth — just the carpet of needles and a few shrubs — and as they climbed higher into the hills, Ace led Will off the trail and into the heart of the woods!

"Wow!" Will gasped as they took air to leapfrog a small ravine that stood in their way. "This is unbelievable! But are you sure we're not damaging the forest floor?"

Ace turned to him in disbelief. His bike wobbled under him as he waited for Will to catch up. "Damaging the forest floor?" he repeated mockingly. "Is that what you said?" He laughed derisively. "Give me a break! You're not one of those tree-hugging enviro-fanatics, are you?"

"Well, no, I've, never actually hugged any trees, but —"

"Whatever's growing on the forest floor will grow back, or it won't," Ace said with a shrug, and pushed on ahead. "Plants don't have feelings, so who cares?"

They crested a hill, and before them, the slope took a steep dive down into a dark ravine. "Yahoooo!" Ace yelled. Will opened his mouth to yell, too. But nothing came out.

The steep grade and the lack of rocks or ruts made this a perfect place to practice downhill riding. Ahead of him, Will saw Ace deliberately spin out, creating a terrible scar in the soft earth at the bottom of the slope.

"Man, you're going to ruin the run!" Will complained.

"Shut up! You don't know what you're talking about!" Ace retorted. "I've been doing this a lot longer than you, and I know a lot more about it. So don't tell me what to do, okay? Not ever!"

Will was shocked into silence. Ace turned around and shoved off down the wide path that bordered the stream at the bottom of the canyon.

"This is the canyon trail," he shouted back over his shoulder. "It's a horseback riding trail, so the trick is to avoid the booby traps! Ha, ha!" He swerved crazily to avoid a pile of horse droppings. Another rut was dug deeply into the horse trail.

Will tried to avoid the droppings, too, but was careful not to do any damage to the trail.

Ace disappeared around a bend. Seconds later, Will heard the frightened whinny of a horse and a child's scream. A man's bellowing, angry voice followed.

Will got off his bike and walked it forward, sensing what had happened and not wanting to have anyone's anger at Ace directed toward him.

"Did you see that?" the man was saying over and over again. He sat astride a big brown horse, and a little girl of about eight, his daughter, Will guessed, sat on a white horse, crying. Her father held the reins of both horses in one hand and had his other arm around the little girl. Next to them were three other riders, all sympathizing.

"They ought to ban mountain bikers from the trails," one of the others said. "Little Michelle practically got thrown! She could've been seriously hurt!"

Just then the man caught sight of Will. He turned on him angrily.

"I'm sorry about him," Will said hurriedly before the man could speak. "But you know, not all mountain bikers act like that. In fact, most of us don't. So I hope you won't hold what happened against all mountain bikers."

"Hmm," the father said, giving his daughter a comforting squeeze. "Well, I'm glad to see somebody's got a little consideration. Listen, do you know the name of that kid?" he asked.

"Um, no," Will said. He balked at getting Ace in trouble. On the other hand, he was going to have to say something to him, even if it meant Ace didn't want to be his friend anymore.

In fact, now that Will thought of it, how good a friend had Ace turned out to be? With his wild behavior at school, he'd gotten the whole club in trouble. And with his antics on the trails, he was giving all mountain bikers a bad reputation.

Will apologized again and rode off after Ace. On

his way, he passed a gum wrapper and two candy wrappers thrown along the trail. When he caught up to Ace, he was chewing gum, and the side of his mouth was stained with chocolate.

"Want some gum?" Ace asked. "What took you? Hit some booby traps?" He laughed, but Will sensed it was a nervous laugh.

Will shook his head. "I'd better get home," he said. "My folks will be wondering where I've gone."

"This place is the best, isn't it?" Ace asked as he strapped on his helmet. Then he shoved off down the trail.

"Yeah. It sure is," Will said. He wondered how long it would stay that way if people like Ace Diamond kept ruining it for everybody.

Will thought suddenly of Danny. Someone had ruined mountain biking for Danny before he'd even gotten started. And from all he'd seen of Ace in the past weeks, he was pretty sure that someone had been him. But he'd never know positively.

One thing he did know, though. Danny was a true friend and a good human being. He always had been.

Will stared at Ace's back as he pedaled down the

trail. If only it were Danny he was biking with, he thought. He wished he could show his pal all the places Ace had shown him.

Then and there, Will made up his mind. He was going to apologize to Danny — for everything. And one last time, he was going to try to talk him into going mountain biking.

9

After school on Monday, Will found Danny at his usual seat in the library. Danny was scribbling away in one of his notebooks, copying information out of a history book about ancient Babylon.

"Man," Will said, grinning and shaking his head. "I wish I had you for a history teacher!"

Danny looked up and could not repress a sly grin. "I don't know all that much," he said modestly.

"More than Mr. Singer, for sure!" Will said, plopping his book bag down on the table and sitting across from his old friend.

"Well, that's not hard," Danny shrugged. He shut his book, first making sure he'd bookmarked the page. "What are you doing here?" he asked. "I thought you had biking club on Monday afternoons." Then he shifted uncomfortably in his seat.

"Oh, yeah, that's right. I forgot. The club's on suspension. I guess I'm responsible for that, right?"

"It wasn't your fault," Will offered. "It was whoever sprayed that graffiti. That was the last straw."

Danny shrugged. "Well, it's nice of you not to hold a grudge," he said. "I hear Mr. Rivera's going to lift the suspension this week anyway." Then he blew out a deep breath and said, "Listen, Will, I'm sorry if I haven't been exactly friendly to you."

"Oh, that's okay," Will said quickly. "I deserve it. I mean —"

"No, it wasn't your fault what that jerk Ace Diamond said to me," Danny pointed out.

"I should have said something," Will insisted. "He was being an idiot, and I feel bad that I didn't stick up for you."

Danny looked down at the table. "That would have been nice, but I understand," he said softly. "It's hard for me to realize sometimes how important it is for some people to be popular."

"But that isn't it!" Will protested.

"It isn't?"

"Not really, no. I don't care about being popular. Not that much anyway. Not if it means you won't want to be my friend. It's just that, well, I joined the mountain biking club, right?"

"Don't remind me."

"And all the kids there happen to be really popular, it's true," Will admitted. "But I just want to have mountain biking buddies, you know? I mean, if you went biking with me —"

"Forget it," Danny cut in, frowning.

"So what was I supposed to do?" Will asked. "If I stuck up for you, Ace would think I was a dork —"

"Oh, thank you very much," Danny commented dryly.

"C'mon, you know what I mean, Danny," Will said. "If I crossed Ace, I'd be, like, out with the club, and I was afraid for that to happen. The rest of the gang is really nice. You'd like them. Especially Gail."

"Uh-huh." Danny didn't sound convinced, but at least he was listening.

"Anyway," Will went on, "it turns out that Ace is a complete jerk."

"I could have told you that," Danny said, smirking. "Go on."

"He rides like a maniac, litters everywhere he goes, messes up the bike paths. He also does some dangerous stuff — yells and screams and scares hikers and horseback riders. In fact, he might even have been one of the kids who nearly ran over us that time. I don't know for sure, but I would bet money on it."

Danny nodded slowly but didn't say anything.

"And I have a feeling that he's the one who sprayed the graffiti, too. So what I'm trying to say is, I'm not going to go riding alone with Ace anymore, even if it means I don't ride on weekends."

"That's all you're trying to say?" Danny prodded him.

"And, well, I'd really like it if — if you would try mountain biking once. And before you say no, just listen for one minute. This is me talking, Danny. Me. Will. And I'm telling you, mountain biking is the most fun thing I've ever done in my entire life! I know you'll like it if you let yourself try it."

"Well," Danny said, making a face but clearly softening, "maybe I'll give it one try. But not with the club. I'm not going anywhere near that maniac."

"Like I said, there are other people in the club, and they're pretty nice — for popular kids, that is."

They both laughed, real friends again for the first time in weeks.

"I could go with you on Saturday," Danny said, giving in. "But I'm not going anywhere dangerous, and if you take me anyplace like that or bring any of your new buddies with you, I'm turning right around."

"Deal!" Will said, grinning from ear to ear. "You won't regret this, Danny. I promise you!"

"I regret it already," Danny said, shooting him a wry look before opening his book again. "Now sit down and do your homework."

Just as Danny had foretold, Mr. Rivera revoked the suspension of the mountain biking club on Thursday morning. They were free to meet on Friday afternoon for the first time in a week.

This posed a minor problem for Will. He didn't want to let Ace know his new intentions. But what if Ace asked him to go riding on Saturday? Will knew that if that happened, he'd have to make up some excuse. But then he would have to disguise the fact that he was going biking with Danny instead.

To make things even more complicated, he

needed to borrow a mountain bike for Danny, since his friend didn't have anything close to suitable. How was Will going to do that?

The only person he could think to ask was Gail Chen, who wasn't very fond of Ace and was ultra-generous. Will felt sure Gail could keep his secret. But she was at least a foot taller than Danny, and her bike would never fit him. Will remembered what Julian down at the bike shop had said about bikes fitting their riders. The last thing Will wanted to do was endanger his best friend.

The bike club met after school, and all the club members were totally psyched to ride after a week of suspension. Only Ace still seemed to have a chip on his shoulder. "Can you believe we're still on probation?" he said, shaking his head in disgust. "One more little tiny incident and the club gets disbanded!"

"You know, Ace," Juliette said, "that's totally in our control. We don't have to provoke any little tiny incidents." The tone of her voice showed in no uncertain terms that she blamed Ace for the club's getting suspended in the first place.

"Look, Mr. Rivera was prejudiced against biking

117

from the beginning!" Ace protested. "How come he didn't suspend those other kids for their petition?"

"Petitioning is legal," Gail commented. "Graffiti is not."

"Are you saying something?" Ace asked. "If you are, just say it, okay?"

"Never mind," Gail said. But the happy mood of the club members had been shaken. Their spirits didn't improve until they were out on the ski trails at Slide Mountain, where they all got caught up in the thrill of riding.

It was a long, wonderful late October afternoon — cool enough so they didn't get too tired. Will wondered if Danny would like it better here or if he should take him somewhere else — like to the ramps, or the South Fork Reservation. There were so many great trails around Montwood that it was hard to choose!

Just then, Ace came up to him. "Hey, kid," he said. "Wanna go back to the state forest tomorrow?"

"No, thanks," Will said. "Umm . . . my parents don't want me biking anymore outside of the club. They got really mad last weekend when they found out I went riding without their permission."

"Man," Ace said, frowning and shaking his head. "Parents can be so unfair! That is just plain mean."

"I know," Will agreed, feeling guilty already about dragging his parents into this little lie of his. "It bites."

"Sure you can't sneak out?" Ace asked hopefully.

"Nah, I'd better not," Will said. "Sorry."

"S'okay," Ace said. "I'll find somebody else to go with."

Will didn't doubt that. Ace always managed to find people to do things with. That was why Will had been so flattered when Ace called for him all those times. He realized, with a start, that Ace's popularity had mattered to him after all. Well, that was over now, whether Danny took up mountain biking or not.

On the way back to town, Will rode his bike up beside Gail's. "Hi!" he said, giving her a little wave.

"How's it goin'?" Gail asked, showing her infectious, braces-covered smile.

"Okay, I guess," Will said. "Actually, there's this friend of mine I'd like to get into mountain biking."

"Cool!" Gail said. "I'm getting tired of the same old faces around here, know what I mean?"

"Yeah." Will nodded in agreement. "Anyway, this friend of mine needs to borrow a bike for Saturday."

"Want to use mine?" Gail asked.

"Thanks, but yours is too big for him."

"Why don't you ask Mitch?" she suggested. "He's not too big. And he and Candy always go away weekends."

"I know," Will said. "But I don't want to let any of the others know about this. See, this kid, he sort of hates Ace's guts."

"Oh." Gail nodded sagely. "Well, hey, I've got an idea! Go borrow a bike from Julian."

"Julian?" Why hadn't he thought of it? Sure! Hadn't Julian said to come see him if he ever needed any help?

On the other hand, Julian worked at Diamond Cycle. Ace Diamond was in there all the time and might show up when he was there. Should he risk going down there this evening?

The way Will looked at it, he had no other choice. It was either get a bike for Danny to ride or lose this golden opportunity, maybe forever. "Thanks, Gail," he said. "You're the best!"

"I know it," Gail said. "What are you all going to do without me when I graduate in January?"

"You're going to graduate in January?"

"Unless I fail something, and I don't think that's going to happen."

"But who'll be club president?"

"I don't know," Gail said. "I guess you guys will have an election. But if you want me to guess, I'd say Ace looks like a shoo-in."

Will frowned. He knew she was right. And if Ace was the club president, forget about Danny ever joining.

Oh, well. He'd just have to cross that bridge when he came to it. For the moment, he had more important things to do, like borrowing a bike from Diamond Cycle without Ace Diamond finding out!

"Hey, dude!" Julian greeted him when Will walked into Diamond Cycle that evening. His mom had kindly dropped him off. She seemed happy for him — glad both that the club had been reinstated and that Will was getting together with Danny again. Apparently, it was a relief to her.

"Hi," Will greeted the older boy, matching his gap-toothed grin with a smile of his own. "Is Ace around?"

"Ace? No. Why, are you looking for him?"

"No! Just the opposite," Will corrected him. "It's . . . I don't want him to see me here tonight."

"Whoa. Cloak and dagger," Julian joked, chuckling. "What's the big secret, if you don't mind my asking?"

"It's just that I told Ace I couldn't go biking with him tomorrow, because I'm actually planning to go biking with someone else. So if he sees me here . . ."

"What exactly are you doing here?" Julian asked. "You didn't ride your bike over to have it retuned, I notice. Are you shopping for something newer and fancier already?"

"It's not for me," Will said. "My friend Danny needs a bike for tomorrow. Not to buy. Like, to borrow."

"Aaaaah," Julian said, nodding knowingly with a sly smile. "And you come to me for help? No prob, dude. I'm sure we can find a bike his size and let him test-ride it for a day or two."

"Fantastic!" Will said, high-fiving Julian. "Are you sure it's okay? What if Mr. Diamond finds out?"

"Hey, it's better than Ace test-riding one," Julian said. "Your friend can't smash them up any faster than him, whatever he does."

"I don't know," Will said. "He's never been mountain biking before."

"Hey, neither had you when you started out," Julian pointed out. "And that wasn't so long ago."

"I just wish Danny and Ace didn't hate each other's guts so much," Will said with a sigh.

"Ah, I see trouble ahead," Julian said. "Gotta work that one out in your mind beforehand."

"I know," Will said. "I'm trying. But nothing's coming to me."

"Something will," Julian assured him. "Just give it time. Meanwhile, let's go pick your friend out a bike!"

10

This thing looks dangerous," Danny commented as he surveyed the bike Will had borrowed for him. It was resting on its kickstand in the center of Will's driveway, and Danny was walking slow circles around it, bending now and then to inspect different parts of it that were evidently mysteries to him.

"Bikes aren't dangerous," Will corrected him. "Riders are. So don't worry. I'm sure you're not going to throw all caution to the wind your first time out."

"Yeah, that's me," Danny grinned. "A real daredevil on wheels. Do I get a helmet and pads, too?"

These Will had borrowed from Gail on Friday after their ride. With minor adjustments to the helmet straps, they fit Danny fine. He always did have a big head for his body, Will reflected.

Danny looked kind of awkward on the bike at first. He never rode anymore, as he told Will. He had never gotten into regular biking as a little kid. "I could never understand why these things don't fall over," he told Will as they rode around the block once or twice for practice. "I mean, a table with only two legs crashes pretty fast."

"You're in motion, duh!" Will shot back, laughing. He knew Danny was making jokes at his own expense. Probably he was doing it so nobody else would be the first to make fun of him. But Will would never have done that, to Danny or anyone else. He knew, of course, that there were plenty of kids who made fun of other kids. It made Will mad that he never had the guts to tell them to shut up.

"So where are you taking me?" Danny said when it was finally time to strap on their day packs and go. The packs were filled with their lunch, and a few tools and spare parts just in case. During his weeks in the club, Will had learned how to prepare for a day-long ride.

"South Fork Reservation," Will told him. He'd thought about taking Danny to the ramps, where they wouldn't meet any hikers or horseback riders.

But the ramps were pretty challenging, and after watching Danny struggle his way around the block, Will decided against taking him there.

Besides, there were bound to be lots of mountain bikers at the ramps. He didn't want to run into Ace or any of the club members who would tell Ace he'd been out biking. Not after he'd lied about it.

"The reservation? I've been there a couple of times for class picnics," Danny said.

"Yeah, but that's only a little corner of it," Will told him. "That's the great thing about mountain biking — you can go everywhere and cover a lot more ground than if you were on foot."

"We'll see," Danny said. But Will could see that his friend was already looking more confident on the bike.

"That bike looks good on you!" Will told him, grinning.

"Aw, be quiet," Danny said, shaking his head but smiling.

It was a perfect biking day, sunny but not too hot, with a slight breeze whistling in the treetops. Will was feeling on top of the world as he turned off the

126

road and into the reservation, leading Danny onto the wide dirt road.

"Uh-oh, here we go!" Danny said, suddenly wobbly as he hit a pothole. "Whoa!" He went over with the bike, hopping away just before it hit the ground.

"You okay?" Will asked.

"No problem," Danny assured him. "I just got spoiled by riding on paved roads all the way here."

"Yeah, gotta watch out for those potholes," Will joked.

"Okay, lead on," Danny said, getting back onto his bike.

Will did, heading off the main dirt road onto a smaller one, and then onto one of the reservation's main trails. It was a well-traveled path, and pretty smooth except for the occasional tree root or steep hill. Will had been on it before, the day the club had come here, and he had liked it then, back when he was a beginner. He figured it would be just right for Danny.

"Whoa!" Danny shouted behind him. Will braked and looked back to see Danny on the ground again.

"You okay?" Will asked.

"Yup. I can see I've got a talent for falling," Danny quipped.

"It comes with the territory," Will assured him. He had even seen Ace fall once or twice, and he thought of mentioning this fact to Danny but decided not to. The mere mention of Ace's name might be enough to spoil the mood for his old friend.

In the next fifteen minutes, Danny fell five more times. But he seemed to be enjoying himself — more and more as the time went by.

After about half an hour, they stopped for a quick drink and then rode on. This time, they went twenty minutes without Danny falling even once.

"You're getting good on that thing!" Will encouraged him.

"Not bad, not bad," Danny said with a self-satisfied grin. "Hey, I'm hungry. All this exercise is giving me an appetite!"

"Cool. Let's eat," Will said. They had stopped by a bench, and now they opened up one of their packs and pulled out the fruit and sandwiches they had brought along.

"Ah, peanut butter and jelly. Gourmet!" Danny said, holding it up to admire.

Will munched on his tuna salad sandwich and smiled. This is pretty perfect, he thought. Out on his bike on a beautiful day, on an excellent trail, with his best friend for company.

Yes, Danny was his true friend, Will realized, in a way that Ace Diamond could never be. Will felt like he could be himself with Danny and could enjoy Danny for who he was.

"So, Dan," he ventured, "how do you like it so far?"

Danny scrunched up his face as though he were thinking hard about it. "Well," he said, "my rear end is a little sore, but what really hurts is admitting I was wrong."

"It's fun, right?" Will prodded. "What did I tell you?"

"Don't rub it in," Danny said. "I hate people who say 'I told you so.'"

"I told you so," Will said.

"I hate you," Danny said.

And they both burst out laughing.

On the way back, Danny couldn't stop talking about how great mountain biking was. "You know what's really great about this," he said excitedly in his funny, nasal voice. "You really get to cover a lot of ground. Like, with hiking, we could have walked for three days to cover the ground we did today."

"That's right," Will said. But he didn't say "I told you so" this time.

"I don't think people understand mountain biking," Danny said. "I know I didn't."

They were riding single file now, with Will trailing. He figured it would boost Danny's riding confidence to let him take the lead.

"You were just angry about nearly getting run over," Will reminded him.

"Yeah, but for instance, we were out all day today," Danny said, "and there must have been fifty bike riders out there, but none of them did anything stupid or dangerous. I thought all bikers rode like maniacs."

"You thought I would ride like that?" Will asked, a little hurt. Danny didn't answer, and Will thought back to the rides he'd taken with Ace Diamond. He'd done some pretty stupid things just to go along with Ace.

"You know what would be good?" Danny asked. Without waiting for a reply, he said, "It would be good if the club would sponsor a 'get acquainted' day."

"A what?" Will asked.

"You know, like public relations. You throw a little party, with free stuff and maybe a little brochure about mountain biking. Mostly it's so you can show people you're not a bunch of idiots with no manners. Tell them a little about how great mountain biking is, and listen to what they have to tell you, too. Some of their complaints might be worth hearing."

Will shook his head in admiration. "You've got to join the club, Danny," he said.

"Forget it," Danny said quickly.

"No, listen," Will insisted. "Those are great ideas. I think the club should do it. So you've got to at least come to the meeting and tell them about it."

"Why can't you tell them?" Danny asked.

"It's your idea," Will said. "Besides, you say it better than I would. I'll back you up. I promise — not like that other time," he added, remembering the incident in the library.

"I don't need to be in the club," Danny said. "I'll just go biking with you on weekends."

"Does that mean you're going to buy a mountain bike?" Will asked hopefully.

"Well, gee, yeah — I guess I'll have to," Danny said. "Hey, it's my birthday in two weeks! I'll just grovel and beg for my parents to get this one for me!"

"You like that one?" Will asked.

"Definitely," Danny said. "I'm comfortable on it already. Who knows if I could even *ride* another one!"

"Come on, they're not that different," Will said with a laugh. "Hey, I'll get you your own elbow and knee pads for your birthday."

"Will," Danny said, suddenly coming to a stop at the side of the road.

Will pulled up beside him. "What's up, Dan?" he asked. "You okay?"

"Listen," Danny said, looking at Will intently. "Just because I'm into mountain biking now, that doesn't mean I'm joining the club at school. 'Cause I'm not."

"Danny, try it, okay?" Will begged. "You've got to

132

admit, I was right about mountain biking. So trust me on this one, all right?"

Danny was silent for a moment. "I'll come to one meeting," he finally said. He shoved his bike back into motion. "But I'm not promising to join. And don't try to talk me into it."

"I won't," Will promised, riding after Danny with a wide grin on his face — and his fingers firmly crossed.

11

The moment he saw it, Will knew he would never forget the look on Ace Diamond's face when Danny showed up for the club meeting on Monday afternoon. Ace had the expression of someone who has just been teleported from a biking club meeting to an alien planet in another galaxy.

"What . . . is going on?" Ace finally managed to say.

"Guys, I'd like to introduce you to Danny Silver, my best friend," Will said pointedly.

Everyone else said hi to Danny, and he nodded back, avoiding Ace's gaze.

"I've been getting Danny into mountain biking," Will told them, "and I wanted him to share with you some of the ideas he came up with for us."

"What?" Ace asked, blinking in disbelief. "When

134

was this? Correct me if I'm wrong, but aren't you the kid who wrote that petition that got us suspended?"

"The petition didn't get the club suspended," Danny shot back. "Spray-painting the school walls had something to do with it."

Ace tensed, and so did Danny. "My point is," Ace said, "that you tried to get us in trouble. You tried to make it so we couldn't go biking anywhere."

"Not *just* anywhere," Danny corrected him. "I still think mountain bikers have to realize they don't own the trails. But I'm not against mountain biking. Not anymore. Will took me out riding this weekend and kind of got me into it."

Will winced. Danny had blown his secret, and Ace shot Will a look of betrayal. Will looked down at the floor.

"So you're, like, not against mountain biking anymore?" Gail asked.

"No," Danny said, glancing at her shyly. "Actually, I think I could get into it."

"You know," Gail said, "I'm the editor of the school newspaper, and it would really help us if you would write, like, a letter to the editor saying you were wrong about mountain biking."

Everyone looked at Danny. He bit his lip, nodded, and said, "Okay. I'll do that. I was wrong, and I guess I have to admit it to everyone."

"You would do that?" Juliette asked, clearly impressed. "Hey, you're okay."

"Yeah," Candy agreed.

Ace spat on the ground. "Dork," he muttered under his breath.

"Shut up, Ace. He is not," Will quickly said.

"Did you just tell me to shut up?" Ace asked disbelievingly.

"Sorry," Will said. "And I'm sorry I wasn't up front with you about what I was doing this weekend. But Danny is not a dork. And he's not a loser. He may not be able to ride like you, and maybe he isn't as cool or as popular, but I know one thing. He would never be reckless on the trail, or scare hikers or horseback riders, or litter, or be mean to somebody just for the fun of it."

There was dead silence from everyone. All eyes went from Will to Ace and back again.

"So — so what are you saying?" Ace asked, at a loss for a comeback.

"I guess what I'm saying is, I want Danny in the club."

"Huh?" Danny said, taken by surprise. "Wait a minute —"

"Forget it!" Ace shouted. "If he's in the club, I'm out!"

"Ace!" Gail said. "Last time I checked, I was still president of this club. And the rule has always been that anyone who wants to join can."

"I don't want to join anyway!" Danny broke in.

"You don't?" Juliette asked. "Why not?"

Danny glanced at Ace. "I just don't — that's all," he said. Turning to Will, he flashed him an angry glance.

"Sorry," Will said.

"I just came because Will said I should tell you about my idea for the club."

"Oh, yeah?" Gail said. "What idea?"

"I thought that, since a lot of people are all weird about mountain biking because some mountain bikers act like jerks," he looked pointedly at Ace, "you guys should have an event to change people's opinions."

"Like a public relations event," Will put in.

"Yeah," Danny said. "Try to show them that you're thinking about everyone and not just yourselves."

"I think that is the dorkiest idea I ever heard," Ace said with a derisive laugh. "Like anybody would come."

"They would if you plan it right," Danny insisted. "You could offer free food and drinks and give out a flyer listing all your plans for improving things."

"What plans?" Steve asked. "We don't have any plans."

"Well, we need to make some, then," Juliette said. "I think we should say, 'We know some bikers don't go by the rules, but we don't accept that.' We could adopt a set of club rules to avoid conflicts on the trails. And to join the club, you'd have to sign a form promising to be courteous to whoever shares the trail."

"Great idea!" Gail said. "We could hand out copies of the rules at the event. But I think we still need something to make it special."

"Hey!" Candy said. "What if we ask for donations

to help pay for trail repairs, to mend some of the damage bad riders cause?"

"Fantastic!" Gail said. "And we could have a raffle, too!"

"And maybe a little biking demonstration from Ace," Mitch suggested.

"Oh, no!" Ace said. "Leave me out of your stupid plan. I'm not doing demonstrations for anybody, and I'm not signing any bunch of rules, either."

"Ace, if we vote the rules in, you'll have to go along with them if you want to stay in the club."

"What do we need a bunch of rules for?" Ace complained. "I say we should have the freedom to ride on any trail we want, anytime we want! Nobody can tell us what to do!"

"It isn't a matter of anybody telling you what to do," Danny said. "It's a matter of agreeing to it yourselves."

"Yeah, well, I'm not agreeing to anything," Ace insisted.

"I say we vote on whether to draw up a new set of rules to regulate biking behavior," Gail said.

"I second the motion," Will said, raising his hand.

"I third it," Juliette said.

"Okay, have a vote," Ace said. "You'll lose anyway. Right, guys?" He turned to Steve and Mitch, but both of them looked down at their shoes.

"I don't know, Ace," Steve said. "It sounds like a good idea to me. Especially if Mr. Rivera knows about it. He won't be looking to suspend the club anymore."

"Yeah," Mitch agreed. "If we tell people we're not going to bother them, then maybe they won't bother us anymore."

"What? I can't believe you guys!" Ace was livid. "What about you?" he asked Candy.

"I . . . I don't know," she said, biting her lip.

"Fine!" Ace said, steaming. "That's just fine. You can take your new rules and sign them, but count me out! I quit this stupid club, and I'll tell you what else — without me, you guys are nothing!"

He grabbed his bike and rode off. Nobody tried to stop him, not even Steve or Mitch.

"He'll get over it," Candy said, not sounding too sure of herself. "He's just mad."

"He's always mad," Gail said. "I guess he has problems he's got to work out on his own. But I think this club can live without him. As long as nobody else quits."

She looked hard at Steve and Mitch. The two boys looked at each other.

"You staying?" Mitch asked Steve.

"I guess so," Steve said.

"Me, too," Mitch said.

"Danny?" Will asked, turning to his friend.

"What?" Danny asked. "I told you —"

"Yes, but you said it was because of Ace," Will pointed out. "Ace just quit."

"He might change his mind and decide to come back," Danny said.

"If he does, he'll have to agree to the rules and to accept that you're in the club," Gail said. "That is, if you want to be in. I hope you do." She smiled at him, and Danny blushed beet red.

"Me, too," Candy said. "That was a good idea you had. I think we should do it. I could bake some cookies and stuff."

Danny looked from one face to the other. "You guys really want me in the club?" he asked.

"Sure!" Juliette said.

"Mitch? Steve?" Danny asked, trying to gauge their reaction.

Steve shrugged. "Okay with me, I guess. Whatever."

"Same here," Mitch said.

"Welcome to the club, Danny!" Gail said, sticking out her hand for him to shake. "I hereby appoint you head of the event committee!"

Danny blinked, totally speechless for once in his life.

"I think we need something to call the event," Juliette said. "You know, a catchy name."

"How about Biker Courtesy Day?" Will suggested.

"If we're raising money for trail repair, we could call it the Repairathon," Danny suggested, recovering his voice.

"Repairathon — that's excellent!" Gail enthused. "Like, it's about repairing relations *and* repairing trails! I'm going up to the school newspaper office to write out some notices right now!"

"I'll help you!" Juliette said. "Come on, everyone — we can write out the new rule sheet and the brochure!"

They all trooped up to the newspaper office, full of energy and excitement. "Hey!" Mitch said as they all sat down to work. "What about our bike ride? Weren't we going to go riding today?"

"It can wait till Wednesday," Gail said, already starting to type at the computer keyboard. "We've got work to do!"

12

The Repairathon was put together in record time. When the club members went to Mr. Rivera with their plan on Tuesday morning, he was thrilled and promised to help get the word out. They decided to hold the event a week from Saturday, to give people enough time to hear about it. The Thursday edition of the school paper trumpeted the news as well.

When the day arrived, the entire school campus was given over to the big event. There was a table with free cookies and soft drinks, a raffle to benefit trail repair, brochures about biking etiquette and safety, with a list of the club's rules included, and lots of other handouts, too. And there was a suggestion box for anyone who wanted to say their piece.

There were several attractions the club had planned for the big event. Since Ace had made himself unavailable to do a biking demonstration, Gail and Will asked Julian to come and give a talk about how to keep a bike in good repair. Julian also brought half a dozen beautiful bikes with him. Mr. Diamond had agreed to sponsor the event on condition that some of his bikes were put on display.

Ace had objected, but his father had had the last word, saying that it would help sell bikes, and that was that.

A local rock band composed of eighth graders played songs about freedom and the open road. And the club members spent their time talking to anyone they could collar about how great mountain biking was and how things were going to be different now between bikers and nonbikers.

The Repairathon committee had added another event during the week as well: a trail litter pickup. The club members had let everyone know that they were going out on their bikes the next day with plastic garbage bags, to pick up whatever trailside litter they could find.

"How much have we brought in?" Will asked Danny and Gail. Over a hundred people had shown up for the Saturday event, and Will thought that each had contributed from two to ten dollars toward trail repair. Gail and Danny were counting up the money as the day's festivities were coming to an end.

"Let's see," Danny said. "Exactly four hundred twenty-two dollars and fifty cents!"

"Awesome!" Gail said, writing down the number. "Man, this is great — I can't believe we didn't think of doing this before!"

"We signed up five new members for the club," Will informed them. "Juliette has the rule sheets they signed."

"Cool!" Gail bubbled. "Hey, Will, when I graduate, I know who I'm nominating as club president. You!"

"Me?" he said, shocked. "I only started a couple months ago, and I'm not that good."

"Who cares?" Gail asked. "Look how much you've brought to the club. We're not hated by everybody anymore, we've got a bunch of new members, we're gonna have clean trails, and best of all, you brought us Danny!"

"Yeah," Will agreed. "Once everybody saw that the writer of the petition was in the biking club, it kind of made people think again about us."

Danny beamed at them. "I can't believe I hated mountain biking," he said. "What a dork I was."

"Nah," Will said. "You were just misinformed — that's all." And the three friends shared a laugh.

Just then, Will spotted his parents over by the coffee machine the club had borrowed for the occasion. "Hey, Mom! Dad!" he called out, waving. Turning to Gail and Danny, he excused himself, saying, "I want to go see how they're doing."

He ran over to where they were standing. "Hi, Mom. Hi, Dad," he said. "Pretty amazing day, huh?"

"Son," his father said, "we're both so proud of you. You had a problem about what to do with yourself after school, and look what a great solution you came up with!"

"I guess so," Will admitted with a shy grin.

"Will," his mother added, "I have to say, I never thought things would turn out so well. Congratulations, honey!" And she gave him a big kiss on the cheek. Will was too happy even to wipe off the lipstick she left behind.

"And you know, Will," his dad said, "your mom and I have been talking. We've decided that you were right — we've been working too much and not spending enough time with you."

"Aw," Will said, "I didn't mean to give you a hard time about that."

"No, you were right," his mother said. "We deserved it. So each of us is going to leave work early one day a week. That way, you won't have to spend afternoons in the library anymore."

Suddenly Will realized that in the weeks he'd been mountain biking, he'd changed his attitudes. "I've actually come to like the library, to tell you the truth," he admitted. "Oh, don't get me wrong — I'd rather spend the time with you guys. But I really like reading now."

"We noticed," his dad said with a sly grin.

"Do you realize," his mother asked, "that you haven't watched TV or played a computer game in weeks?"

Will had to laugh, "No," he said, looking around at all the new mountain bikes on display, "I guess I haven't!"

Matt Christopher®

Sports Bio Bookshelf

Lance Armstrong

Kobe Bryant

Terrell Davis

Julie Foudy

Jeff Gordon

Wayne Gretzky

Ken Griffey Jr.

Mia Hamm

Tony Hawk

Grant Hill

Ichiro

Derek Jeter

Randy Johnson

Michael Jordan

Mario Lemieux

Tara Lipinski

Mark McGwire

Greg Maddux

Hakeem Olajuwon

Shaquille O'Neal

Alex Rodriguez

Briana Scurry

Sammy Sosa

Venus and
Serena Williams

Tiger Woods

Steve Young

Read them all!

*Previously published as *Crackerjack Halfback*

Look Who's Playing First Base

Miracle at the Plate

Mountain Bike Mania

No Arm in Left Field

Nothin' But Net

Olympic Dream

Penalty Shot

Pressure Play

Prime-Time Pitcher

Red-Hot Hightops

The Reluctant Pitcher

Return of the Home Run Kid

Roller Hockey Radicals

Run, Billy, Run

Run for It

Shoot for the Hoop

Shortstop from Tokyo

Skateboard Renegade

Skateboard Tough

Snowboard Maverick

Snowboard Showdown

Soccer Duel

Soccer Halfback

Soccer Scoop

Spike It!

The Submarine Pitch

Supercharged Infield

The Team That Couldn't Lose

Tennis Ace

Tight End

Too Hot to Handle

Top Wing

Touchdown for Tommy

Tough to Tackle

Wheel Wizards

Windmill Windup

Wingman on Ice

The Year Mom Won the Pennant

All available in paperback from Little, Brown and Company